EMMA CHIZZIT AND THE SACRAMENTO STALKER

Also by Mary Bowen Hall
EMMA CHIZZIT AND THE QUEEN ANNE KILLER

EMMA CHIZZIT AND THE SACRAMENTO STALKER

For Winnie Jensen - Enjoy some more!

Mary Bowen Hall

Mary Bowen Hall

Walker and Company
New York

First published in the United States of America in 1991
by Walker Publishing Company, Inc.
Published simultaneously in Canada by Thomas Allen & Son
Canada, Limited, Markham, Ontario

Library of Congress Cataloging-in-Publication Data

Hall, Mary Bowen.
Emma Chizzit and the Sacramento stalker / Mary Bowen Hall.
p.   cm.
ISBN 0-8027-5777-4
I. Title.
PS3558.A37166E48   1991
813'.54—dc20   90-12878
CIP

Printed in the United States of America
2 4 6 8 10 9 7 5 3 1

In tribute to Sacramento's Barbara Wiedner,
founder of Grandmothers for Peace, and
courageous women activists everywhere.

$\triangledown$

1

"*ROAD TOADS?*" I ASKED incredulously.

"Road toads," Brenda Friedman repeated. "You know what they are."

I knew. Dead toads, flattened and dry. At certain times of year you could find them, run over, on the streets almost anywhere in Sacramento. They're a big item with the junior high school kids.

"I found a box of those damn toads on the doorstep of our new headquarters, just this morning. A big cardboard carton, lots of toads."

Brenda's a women's activist who lives in our neighborhood. She's the founder of an outfit called Jobs First—and hardly a shrinking violet. She'll go up against police barricades, macho hecklers, you name it. I wondered what was so threatening about a box of dried-out toads.

"Why are you worried?" I moved from the bedroom to the kitchen of my little apartment, trailing the phone cord behind me. I thought it was probably some kid prank.

I still felt wary, ready to turn down a pitch to take part in one of Brenda's *actions*. She'd tried before to inveigle me into one thing or another. I wholeheartedly believe women should have equal opportunity when it comes to earning a living, but I don't approve of most of the things Brenda's Jobs

1

First group does. They go too far—particularly when it comes to getting themselves arrested.

Not that Brenda's outfit doesn't do things that tickle my funnybone. They created a big flap last year with a protest against construction workers who didn't want women on the job site—the men were trying to make the female workers quit by monopolizing the toilets. Brenda and company made an early morning raid to install padlocks on the portapotties. They decorated them with pink ribbons tied in huge bows and then, of course, invited the television news reporters to photograph the arrival of the men on the job. But the reaction of some of the men had been nasty, and then the whole thing turned sour, with— as I remembered— arrests on both sides.

"Did you know we opened a new office?" Brenda asked. "We've just moved into it, it's our first real headquarters."

There had been a lot of publicity about the office in the *Sacramento Bee* last week, a big article and several photographs. Maybe that's what had triggered the delivery of the flattened toads.

"Um-hum," I said. I'd begun thinking of ways to say no. We'd never had a conversation yet without Brenda asking me to do something, and if I didn't say no to people like Brenda I'd have no time to call my own. I'm not retired. I can't afford to be. I have my own business, A-1 Salvage, to stretch my Social Security check. I contract to clean out commercial buildings or old houses, most often when someone has died and the family doesn't want to do the clean out on their own. It's a good business. I get paid up front for my labor, and I can sell anything of value I find. On top of my salvage contracts, I do chores for my friend Frannie Edmundson in exchange for my little apartment above her garage. What with one thing and another, what I laughingly call a *normal* day—one with any spare time in it—is a rare treat.

"That box with the toads in it . . ." Brenda laughed, a small brittle sound. "It had a threat written on the side."

"What did it say?"

She hesitated.

" 'Bitches,' and 'Stay home or be flattened.' "

Crude and direct. But maybe not all that ominous.

"It could be just kids messing around," I told her.

I was looking out my kitchen window, down toward the driveway and the accumulation of magnolia leaves under the tree opposite Frannie's porte-cochere. It was time to rake them up again, to save for winter mulch. To my surprise, a big gray Chrysler turned in at our driveway. A man in a chauffeur's uniform and cap was driving.

Brenda laughed another one of those brittle laughs. "I don't know . . . I don't think it's just kids." I was disturbed by the edgy tone in her voice.

The driver got out of the Chrysler and headed for Frannie's front door, carrying a small sheaf of papers. Now what was that all about?

"I . . . there was a threatening phone call to the office yesterday," Brenda said.

She had my attention now—it sounded to me as if she were taking a time-out to make sure she had control of her voice.

"The caller was definitely not a kid. It was a man, with a deep, guttural voice. His talk was . . . nasty, full of anatomical references." She stopped, drew a deep breath. "He had a lot to say about *things* he'd like to do to us. And that's when I thought of calling you. I heard how you solved that killing—the business that started with you finding the dead baby in that old house."

I watched the gray-uniformed chauffeur return empty-handed from Frannie's front door, get in the car and leave. I wished Brenda had never heard about the dead baby in the Queen Anne Victorian—solving that case did *not* confer magical powers on me.

"I'm sure the phone call was from the same person who left the box," Brenda went on. "I named him *toad man*."

"Maybe you should tell the police."

"No . . . not yet. We try to keep a good rapport with law enforcement. You know, every time we have a demonstration we tell them where we'll be and what we'll be doing—even if we're planning civil disobedience. We didn't always get along with them so well, but it's better now. With this kind of a complaint, we might lose more than we'd gain. We have to be taken seriously, not dismissed because somebody thinks we're just a bunch of hysterical women."

I supposed she was right. "What do you want from me?" I asked—words I never thought I'd say to Brenda. But I didn't like the idea that someone was trying to intimidate her and her group.

"Tonight's the Women Take Back the Night rally, and afterward a march to Old Sacramento. You know, they have one every September. Now don't say no—I'm not asking you to march with us, but just be there. Maybe stay nearby."

"You mean, watch over you?"

"Right—exactly."

"Okay." So much for the quiet evening I'd had in mind.

"Thank you! Oh—could you come a little early? I want to introduce you to the others before the rally starts."

I assented reluctantly with the proviso the others not be told about the Queen Anne thing. Now that she had me on the hook, Brenda was going on a mile a minute about the Women Take Back the Night cause.

The Take Back the Night march was another case where I approved of the goal but didn't hold with the method. I can't see the logic of a bunch of women parading around for one night—it doesn't keep women safe the other 364 nights of the year. But I suppose once you have one of these marches scheduled, you have to get as many women as possible to turn out. What if they gave one of these shindigs and hardly anybody showed up?

Brenda was going on full force about the parade, and how a turnout from older women like me was especially needed.

"Support from all segments of the community is absolutely essential. I think it would be just wonderful if you could bring your friend, too. You know, your landlady? Frannie."

Fat chance. Brenda should have figured out by now that Frannie didn't go in for that sort of thing. "I don't think so," I said.

"Well . . . see you tonight at six thirty. Be sure to bring a flashlight." She paused, shifting vocal gears. "And . . . um . . . thank you, Emma."

After I hung up, I got to wondering what kind of trouble I might be able to prevent at tonight's parade. Precious little, it seemed to me.

$\triangledown$

2

T HAT NIGHT I HAD a quick supper and changed into my one-and-only silk shirt and good slacks. Then, flashlight in hand, I pondered my chances of getting past the porte cochere without attracting Frannie's notice. It was early September, but the weather in Sacramento is still warm at this time of year. She'd be inside with the air conditioner going full blast; I thought I'd have a shot at a clean get-away. But I'd scarcely started down the driveway before Frannie appeared at her side door.

"Why, Emma, don't you look nice!"

Frannie always compliments me when I wear something besides my khaki pants and work boots—hoping, I suppose, that I'll change my style. She and I have known each other for a long time, since high school days. She is kindly, generous, and true-blue, and I'm grateful to her for a lot of things—but not for her efforts to *improve* me.

"But where on earth are you going with that flashlight?"

"I'm . . . um . . . going to walk downtown."

I suppose it did look strange, carrying the flashlight while it was still daylight. I had to hoof it, I'd put my old Dodge truck in for repairs. The truck was supposed to have been ready for the weekend, only it wasn't—some parts hadn't come in.

6

Frannie gestured at my flashlight.

"I'm going to the Women Take Back the Night march," I said. "You're supposed to bring a flashlight."

"Oh, Emma!" She was all cat-that-swallowed-the-canary. "You're going to that women's liberation thing!"

"Women's movement." I made the correction automatically. Frannie's never realized the problems a lot of women face. All her life she's done exactly what her mother brought her up to do. She snagged Frank Edmundson for a husband, and he became one of the wealthier members of the California Legislature—after which he had the good grace to die before he got to that age when men trade their wives in for younger models.

Although she's not above enjoying a few frivolous infractions, Frannie's always followed what she believes are *the rules*. She's gotten good results, so she's always puzzled that other women don't do as she's done.

I didn't mention it was Brenda who'd asked me to come to the march. Frannie'd had a lot to say last year when Brenda served jail time for obstructing traffic during a demonstration on the Sacramento State campus. Brenda's theory was that men were blocking women's promotions in one of the conservative campus departments, and so women were entitled to block traffic. I thought it was stretching a point to make the comparison. Why inconvenience a whole bunch of blameless students and university employees?

"Oh, but . . . you're not going to walk downtown?"

"It's not all that far, Frannie. Twelve blocks to get from here to Tenth Street, then another . . . um . . . seven blocks over to the capitol."

"At night? It's absolutely too far!"

"Frannie, that's what this event is supposed to be about."

"Well, certainly, during the march, with all those women there together. But not afterward!"

I wasn't worried. For one thing, I'm tall and broad-shouldered. For another, I step right along. I pride myself on that. You're not going to catch me moving like an *old lady*. Besides, I had my trusty flashlight. It's solid and heavy, made of good old-fashioned metal—I wouldn't own one of those flimsy plastic things.

"I'll be just fine," I told Frannie.

She didn't see things my way. "You're taking the car," she declared.

There was no sense protesting. She was already trotting back toward the house on her short legs, the glossy brown curls of her doll-like hairdo bobbing, her flowered caftan billowing behind her plump body. "I'll be back in two shakes," she called over her shoulder.

I waited, feeling more annoyed by the minute. I'd rather have walked. And now that she was loaning me the Mercedes, she'd think I owed her a full report after the march was over.

She reappeared and thrust the car keys into my hand. "Have fun!"

It didn't seem to me that *fun* was the right word to describe the evening in prospect. And as I backed out of the driveway, I remembered—too late—that I'd forgotten to ask about the big gray Chrysler and the chauffeur.

Downtown, I circled Capitol Park a couple of times looking for a place to park. I should have known, I thought, that the early-bird marchers would already have taken them all. I gave up and drove over to the south side of Capitol Mall, an area full of state office buildings—crowded by day but deserted at night.

I parked and locked the car, pocketed the key, and walked to the Capitol's west steps.

Several television stations were setting up equipment. The steps face toward the setting sun and make a great stage, especially late in the day. The Capitol's portico runs the width of the building and has several ranks of descending steps flanked with dark, tall trees—pines, cedars, and magnolias. A picture perfect scene, so to speak.

Brenda and some of her followers were stationed on the lawn to the right of the steps. She spotted me right away.

"Emma! Emma Chizzit!"

A few heads turned. It happens whenever someone hollers

my name in a crowd. I don't care. I've had the name Emma all my life, but, as my own private joke after a particularly difficult time in my life, I *chose* Chizzit.

Once Brenda had me in tow, she rattled off the names of the women with her—Esther Vajic and her mother Coretta, Kitty Hackett and Anne Krouse.

I'd met Esther before. You couldn't *not* remember Esther. All enthusiasm and dramatic fire—tall and slender, with ivory skin, fantastic gray eyes, and a mane of coal black hair. Tonight she was dressed with a flair befitting a teacher of art at City College: a bright red jumpsuit, fuchsia scarf, and Chinese orange belt, bracelets, and earrings.

Coretta Vajic is more or less an older version of Esther. She has the same sort of looks, and I imagine she once got herself up in much the same way. But now she goes for the *tasteful lady* look. You'd have trouble imagining her involved with anything radical . . . well, maybe a "Beyond War" bumper sticker on her Volvo station wagon.

Our introductions finished, Esther and Brenda went back to a conversation they'd been having about the road toad business.

"I say we ought to wring every ounce of publicity out of it," Esther declared. "It's absolutely right for television. I can *see* it!" She pantomimed placing a box of toads on the lawn beside her. "There it is, on the steps of the office." She swooped close, imaginary camera in hand. "The cameras start on the toads, a close shot. Then they go back to show the lettering on the box . . . back some more to give people a look at our office . . ."

"It's an attention-getter all right," Kitty Hackett interjected. "But do we want more attention just now?"

Kitty's a smart lawyer, I've seen her in action a couple of times. Tonight she was wearing her usual out-of-work-hours uniform: jeans and a sweatshirt with a picture on it. This sweatshirt was blue, with the outline of a mountain peak. Annapurna, I thought; a Sacramento woman led an expedition there some years back. Underneath the outline of the mountain was a slogan: *A woman belongs on top.*

Coretta Vajic made a placating gesture toward her daughter. "What with this threat and all, maybe we shouldn't have worked so hard to get attention for the office in the first place."

Amen, I thought.

All this time the fourth person, Anne Krouse, hadn't said a word. I had the impression she was new to the group. She appeared to be in her mid-thirties, and I was puzzled that she was wearing such harsh, gloomy colors—all wrong for her fair complexion and strawberry blonde hair. She'd favored me with a brief smile when we were introduced, but seemed to be on a real downer. I wondered if the mood were temporary or permanent.

Brenda, of course, is unfailingly cheerful and charming. But then, she's always *on*.

In public, Brenda puts on a demure grandmother persona. She's young for the image, I don't think she's much over fifty. Still, she wears a pair of little glasses on the end of her nose and fixes her hair, which is prematurely white, on top of her head. It's not one of those severe topknots, but a fluffed-out bun, precarious looking. Little tendrils hang down, a la Katharine Hepburn. Tonight she wore a petite moss green dress with ever-so-proper lace collar and cuffs.

The road toad discussion ended, apparently with no conclusion; a woman began making announcements from a microphone set up at the top of the Capitol steps. I divided my attention between the loudspeaker announcements and the view westward down Capitol Mall. The Tower Bridge was silhouetted against the beginnings of a murky sunset; beyond it a red-globe sun was poised to sink into the even redder haze that obscured the western horizon.

Lois Muldoon, another member of Brenda's inner circle, showed up just as the announcer declared a last call to buy T-shirts, buttons, and bumper stickers.

Lois brandished a plain white envelope and a sheet of paper. "I've been by our postal box," she announced in a worried tone. "Someone is sending us hate mail."

"Damn!" Brenda said. "Toads by special delivery and a phone call aren't enough. Now we get a follow-up letter."

She took the sheet of paper and started to read it silently. Kitty and Esther crowded close to look over her shoulder.

Lois shook her head. "I don't think it's from the same source," she said softly.

"Why—what does it say?" Coretta asked.

"It's full of religious talk. We're harlots: we should stay at home. I'm uneasy about the sound of this—a fanatic, perhaps someone who is delusional. I think we should take this very seriously."

Lois is a psychologist, retired now. I figured she knew what she was talking about when it came to the seriousness of a piece of hate mail.

"This is *strange*," Brenda said. "Biblical quotations at the top and bottom."

She held it up. The letter looked as if it had been written on an electric typewriter, or maybe came out of one of those inexpensive letter-quality printers. The passages at the top and bottom were in a different typeface, and centered.

"The message is addressed . . ." Brenda put a mock scowl on her face and dropped her voice a full octave. "It's addressed," she intoned, " 'To the harlots.' "

Lois was frowning and shaking her head. "Take this seriously," she said.

" 'Let this be your warning,' " Brenda went on in the same portentous tones, ignoring Lois. " 'Now you will realize you must purge the evil from amongst you.' "

" '*Now* you will realize?' " Kitty said. "Someone seems to be placing a lot of faith in the effect of this letter."

Brenda continued, the mocking tones fading from her voice. " 'Do you not know what you have done? Why do you let Satan persuade you to meddle in the affairs of men? A woman's place is in the home, unless she goes about the Lord's business.' "

"Read the signature," Lois prodded.

" 'I am the spirit that shall overcome your wickedness.' That's all in caps. And then below there's more from the Bible. Want me to read it?"

Everyone assented.

" 'A wife of noble character is her husband's crown, but a disgraceful wife is like decay in his bones.' It's from Proverbs, says so right here—all the quotes are labeled. And we've got two more, Colossians and Timothy. 'Wives, submit to your husbands, as is fitting in the Lord'—,oh I'm so sick of hearing that—and 'I do not permit a woman to teach or to have authority over a man; she must be silent.' "

"Go back to what's up at the top," Lois said, sounding uncharacteristically grim.

" 'To him who overcomes, I will give the right to eat from the tree of life, which is in the paradise of God.' That's marked as being from Revelations. 'To him who overcomes, I will give the right to sit with me on my throne . . . make a pillar in the temple of my God . . . give authority over the nations . . .' "

"Chapter and verse," Kitty said. "Citations for every quote." She made a wry face. "Complete authorization from on high, duly documented and including a list of rewards for the *spirit that shall overcome*. Overcome our wickedness, I suppose."

Lois looked dismayed. "Don't make fun," she admonished. "Brenda, read the rest up at the top, the final bit."

" 'He will rule them with an iron scepter, he will dash them to pieces like pottery.' "

Dash them to pieces like pottery. Spooky—I wondered if the letter writer literally meant to do something on that order.

Brenda folded the letter slowly. "For now, let's not worry," she said. "We can't do anything about this until after the march."

By this time the sales tables were being folded and the first marchers had begun moving toward Tenth Street. A contingent of high school girls had started a chant:

> Women have the right
> To walk safe at night.

"Let's get going," Brenda said. "Give us the banner, Esther."

Esther handed over a long roll of cloth, heavy green felt, a yard high and three or four yards long. She began to unroll it; Brenda, Kitty, Coretta and Anne stepped forward in turn to grasp the top.

"I've got to leave now," Esther announced. "Mom," she said to Coretta, "take the banner home with you after the parade, okay?"

"Sure. Bye-bye, honey." Coretta turned to me, apparently feeling obliged to apologize for her daughter's departure. "She has to go to an art department function."

Brenda's group took a minute to adjust the way they held the banner, which proclaimed "Jobs First" in bold white letters. I waited on the Capitol lawn as they joined the group on Tenth Street. Things were slow at first, but then the marchers got going, steaming toward J Street and downtown.

I started off a careful distance behind Brenda and company, but first took time for one last westward look down Capitol Mall. The sun had floated far down into the haze and become a squashed-flat orb. It hovered just above the line of hills in the distance, coloring us all with a dull red glare.

▽

3

THE MARCH WAS SCHEDULED to meander along a zig-zag course across the checkerboard of lettered and numbered downtown streets and through the downtown shopping area. Then it would go under the Interstate-5 freeway and into Old Sacramento, where it was to turn around, come back through the underpass, and return to the Capitol.

Through all of this, I was supposed to be keeping an eye out for trouble. I hoped I'd be able to spot some macho type as a possibility for the one who sent the road toad threat, but more likely not. And the Bible-quoting letter writer? No chance.

Nonetheless, I kept my eye on the Jobs First marchers and the crowd surrounding them as they went along the K Street Mall and crossed over to the large open area at Third and J in front of the Holiday Inn, and then through the wide pedestrian underpass. At the turnaround point in Old Sacramento, I stood to one side to watch as the remainder of the marchers emerged from the pedestrian subway and straggled in a disorganized semi-circle. I stood on the cobblestone pavement, uneasy, and watched cars stack up behind the police cruisers positioned at the crosswalks to block traffic for us. The driver of the patrol car directly in front of me stared straight ahead, *no expression* stolidly fixed on his face. I wondered what he thought.

14

I knew what a lot of cops would think, especially Vince Valenti. Vince is a smalltown policeman who took a shine to me when I was involved in that business about the Queen Anne and the dead baby. I've been trying to shake him ever since.

I've never solicited Vince's opinion on the topic of demonstrations—I try never to initiate anything with Old Lonely. But given his views on most other issues, I didn't think he'd have anything favorable to say about this shindig. I could imagine him working a traffic detail at this intersection, standing stalwart and sweaty faced, keeping his back to the marchers. He'd follow orders and stop traffic for them, but he wouldn't like it. "Aw, Emma," he'd say to me afterwards. "Why did you go and get mixed up with *them?*"

Other cars waited behind the patrol cruiser. The twilight was deepening and folks were beginning to turn on their headlights. One or two cars, impatient at having to cool their heels on account of our march, began honking their horns. I was relieved when everyone again started to head through the underpass.

By this time I'd settled on a pattern for watching over the Jobs First marchers. I kept track of faces among the nearby spectators, figuring that I needed to be suspicious of anyone who kept turning up. Until now I'd had an easy time of it, but with darkness coming and the crowds bunching up in the underpass, there wasn't much I could see.

Traffic roared overhead, echoing in the wide concrete-walled subway. Added to the racket was visual noise—murals on the underpass walls that harked back to Diego Rivera and forward to God-knows-who. I scowled at the sharp angles and electric colors. The underpass was brightly illuminated, the vapor-lamp glare making the swirls of purple and yellow look even worse. And, adding to my annoyance, the noise level of the parade itself began to escalate. People who had brought whistles started to blow them; a few hippie types began making long warbling whoops.

A group of marchers began to chant again.

> Women have the right
> To walk safe at night.

Noises in the underpass echoed and re-echoed. In seeming response, the chanting became more shrill. Someone nearby let out a long blast on a police whistle, and, behind me, a little tyke in a stroller began to cry. The poor kid was scared half out of her mind. There was a babysitting service for the marchers; her mother should have had more sense than to put her through this.

I'd had enough.

I shifted speed from *amble* to *get-there*, and started forward through the ranks of marchers, giving Brenda and her group a wide berth and detouring past middle-aged business and professional women struggling along in traditional suits and high heels, hard-core looking gals in masculine clothes, and a group of with-it looking types carrying Sacramento Women's Network signs.

We'd now left J Street and come over to L, and I pushed through the crowd making its way toward the Greyhound station at Seventh and L.

This neighborhood, though much improved in recent years, is still a no-man's land—spittle-smeared sidewalks, empty bottles, trash from take-out restaurants. Human trash, too. I cut behind a police motorcycle, heading for the south side of L Street, and almost tripped over a pair of stuck-straight-out-legs. One of Seventh Street's finest, propped against a mailbox, looked up with bleary eyes. He grinned at me and waggled come-here signals with the hand that held his paper-bag bottle. A *male menace*. I grinned back.

I knew the marchers would continue up L Street, then turn at Ninth and whoop-te-do their way back to the Capitol. I cut away on my own, heading across the Mall and toward the area where I'd parked Frannie's car.

The solitude and silence among the deserted office buildings suited me just fine. I took occasional shortcuts across patches of well-watered lawn, moving through pools of cool air, but mostly stayed to the sidewalks, which exuded a dusty fragrance and held the last of the day's warmth.

I slowed as I neared Frannie's car, enjoying the last faint glow of daylight outlining the western horizon. I was *alone on a dark street*. Frannie would be worried sick if she knew.

$\triangledown$

4

I'D JUST OPENED THE door of Frannie's Mercedes when the man slammed into me like a freight train. We both sprawled sideways across the front seat. He was on top. I was on my right side with his weight full on me and his knees grinding into my thighs.

I clenched my left arm—the one that wasn't pinned under me—tight to my side. He was grabbing, trying to get hold of my wrist.

"Bitch . . . bitch."

His knees ground relentlessly into my legs as he switched from trying to grab my wrist and went for my breast. He squeezed. Hard. I gasped from the pain.

"Bitch . . . gonna *fuck* you."

His knees slid off my thighs, but he maneuvered them right back. He chuckled. It was deliberate, I realized, grinding his knees in. He *used* pain.

I struggled. He maneuvered.

He stank. Gasoline. And I caught another odor. Stale alcohol.

Desperate, I jammed an elbow into his ribs as hard as I could. Where was my flashlight?

He swore, then captured my wrist and twisted my arm, at the same time rising to a kneeling position. Lord! He was

18

fumbling with his pants; his body smell was worse than ever. I managed to snap my arm out of his grasp.

"Bitch!"

He grabbed me by the hair and jerked my head back; I almost lost consciousness from the pain. Another yank on my hair, and then he jammed my face forward into the car seat. I flailed uselessly with my free arm. He was laughing out loud now. He recaptured my wrist, at the same time pushing my face harder into the seat.

His hand was an iron vise. My scalp throbbed. His knees dug and dug.

"Goddam bitch."

He was breathing hard now, in short, labored pants. Except for his breathing there was silence. I could hear nothing, no sound to indicate the possibility of any help nearby. His breath was foul, the overpowering stench of his body filled the car. His breathing, hoarse and ragged, was the only sound accompanying our struggle. The streets were vacant, the office buildings empty.

He took in a quick snuffling breath.

God! I could hear the mucus rattling in his nasal passages.

"Bitch." His grip on my hair loosened.

I was covered with the foul torrent of his exhalations, unable to rid my mind of the sound of that snuffling breath. It conjured up images of bleary men, diseased and filthy, sprawled on spittle-smeared sidewalks, men who hawked and snuffled and spat—infected with every disease imaginable.

He was one of them. I just couldn't let him—

I jerked both arms inward and brought my knees up. I wrenched free, turned onto my stomach, then straightened and pushed back, rearing up as far as I could.

I'd smashed him against the roof of the car. I scrambled backwards on my hands and knees, pushing him toward the still-open door; I heaved backward. He clung to me, breathing curses. I reached down, groped on the car floor for the flashlight until my hand gripped it. I twisted, pushed with my legs, forcing him upward and outward again.

We both fell to the ground, my flashlight clattering onto the pavement.

I got up, found the flashlight, whirled to strike at him. He rolled away from me, and I went after him, flailing with my weapon. But he had his arms up to protect his face; I couldn't land a blow that mattered. Still, I kept hitting, desperate, battering uselessly against his shoulders and arms.

I heard glass tinkling; the lens had broken.

You're supposed to scream, I remembered. There was no one around to help but I cut loose and gave it my best. I backed off and lunged, screaming like a banshee and holding the flashlight with both hands. I swung it in a great arc, blindly.

I felt it connect.

I must have bashed him square in the face. He turned and ran.

I flung myself into the Mercedes and locked the doors. Then, right away, I banged down on each button again to make sure they were all properly locked.

$\triangledown$

5

I HAD TO GET to a safe place, go where there were lights. Lights and people—a restaurant maybe. There was a Carrow's on Tenth, at the corner of S, or maybe it was T.

I'd find it.

My knees were shaking, my hands trembling. I wasn't in any condition to drive, but nevertheless I started the Mercedes and pulled unsteadily from the curb. With the windows up, the smell in the car was overwhelming—stale gasoline, alcohol and sweat. Fighting nausea, I clenched the wheel and drove as far as the corner, where I looked in all directions.

Empty streets. I closed my eyes momentarily in relief.

The car smelled so bad. I was tempted to roll down the windows. No. Frannie had air conditioning. I turned it up full force. When the cool air hit my face, I realized I'd been crying.

I drove slowly, wiping my tears with my sleeve. By God, I'd fought him off! But what if I hadn't? I'd been so lucky, astoundingly lucky. If he'd raped me it might have been a sentence of death—no telling what diseases he had.

I couldn't let myself think about it.

I saw lights ahead, and the big Carrow's sign. I pulled into the restaurant lot, not caring that I'd turned too soon and bumped over the curb. I'd spotted an empty space in front

of the entrance and was determined to park there before
someone else did—I had no intention of parking at the back
end of a dimly lit lot.

The OPEN 24 HOURS sign in the restaurant window cast
a reassuring glow. Inside, I could see a waitress at the cash
register talking with one of the customers. Everything seemed
very everyday, very comforting. I turned off the car lights and
the ignition and looked around. I needn't have hurried for
the parking spot; the lot was only half full, maybe less.

I was okay.

I rolled down all four windows, welcoming the cleansing
freshness of the evening air, and leaned back. My scalp was
sore and my thighs ached. I was going to have some terrible
bruises, I realized. But I was safe.

Who would I have to show the bruises to?

The police, maybe. And if I told anybody else, they'd want
to see. I didn't want to be *examined*, like some damned
exhibit.

I needed to plan what to tell the police.

The man's breath—I steeled myself to remember it exactly. The smell was definitely *stale* alcohol. I'd recognized
the odor immediately. It was not an exhalation of beer or
wine or whiskey, but a smell I knew all too well because I'd
once had to live with it—the fetid, perfumy odor of alcohol
metabolizing from the bloodstream.

I had no idea what the man had been drinking. Fortified
wine was a good bet. I'd been in combat, *mano a mano*, with
a stinking sidewalk wino. *Emma vs. the Seventh Street Kid.*

That dirty, smelly, snuffling man! He'd come *that* close
to getting me. My stomach wrenched. My mind reeled with
images of the bus station sidewalks, smears of spittle, thick
and dark yellow.

I couldn't let myself think about it. I had to get organized.

I fumbled on the car floor for my eyeglasses, found them
on the passenger side, and cleaned them vigorously. The
bastard belonged in jail, I thought. Someone like that
shouldn't—couldn't—be allowed loose.

I fished in the glove compartment for the packaged wipes

Frannie kept there, and gave my face a thorough scrubbing, after which I turned down the visor and scrunched to see myself in the clip-on mirror. As nearly as I could tell by the parking lot lights and the restaurant sign's red neon glow, there was no external sign of what had happened to me. I was the same as ever, long of jaw and nose, a squareset look to my face.

It was time to go inside, to report what had happened to the police.

I'd have to remember to tell them how he smelled—not just the alcohol odor on his breath, but the other smell. It had been on his clothes. It was gasoline, but not fresh gasoline. Maybe musty mechanic's rags. I remembered the long-ago smell of gasoline soaked into dirt, the smell of my grandmother's lean-to garage out behind the barn where she kept the Model T. Funny, after all these years, how vividly and exactly I could recall that smell. Maybe now it would help the police identify the so-and-so. I sat straighter in the car seat, feeling better, ready to get on with the business at hand.

I'd need change for the phone. I checked my pants pocket. Yes, my little wallet was right there. I reached over and unlocked the car door. I was about to open it when my glance happened to land on the ignition. I froze. The keys—I'd been about to leave the car with the keys still in the ignition.

Exactly how non compos mentis was I? I'd let my mind wander, almost left the keys in the car. But I'd come immediately to a place where there were lights and people, and with the car doors locked. I'd checked myself to make sure I was okay, cleaned up a little. I hadn't actually done anything that was a mistake. Yet.

I was struck with an overwhelming desire to go home. Of course! I could call the police from there—much better than going inside, saying what I had to say on the phone in front of a bunch of strangers.

I backed carefully out of the lot, threaded my way through dark and empty streets, and before long turned safely into our shadowed driveway. As silently as I could, I pulled the car past the windows of the den where a flickering glow inside told me Frannie was still watching television. I got the car into the garage quietly, then let myself out the side door even more quietly.

The porte cochere light didn't go on; the television's flickering glow continued unabated. I'd made it—there'd be no inquisition tonight from Frannie.

My apartment is above the garage, with an outside stairway up to it. My cat Sourpuss sat on the little perch at the top of my stairs, waiting. When I reached the porch, he began rubbing back and forth against my ankles. The friendly greeting from my old friend made me feel a great deal better. Sourpuss meowed loudly.

"Sssh!" I whispered, almost giggling. "Do you want Frannie to hear you?" It felt good to be able to joke.

Once I was inside I checked to make sure all the doors and windows were securely locked. After that, I gave Sourpuss a treat, a midnight snack of canned tuna, and then stood there for a moment, stroking him and enjoying my relief at being home.

The message light on my phone in the bedroom was blinking. I went in and sat on the edge of the bed, quite suddenly tired. I massaged my aching thighs and watched the machine's insistently blinking red eye, I don't know for how long. I jumped when the phone rang.

One ring . . . two . . . three. I decided to play possum and let the machine take it.

"Emma?" Frannie's voice. "It's getting sort of late. I was worried." An exasperated little sigh. "Well, I guess you're not home. Let me know if you got in safe and sound, all right? Anytime up until eleven o'clock tonight. Okay? Toodle-oo."

I was annoyed, and at the same time grateful she'd called. She'd roused me from my torpor. I had to call the police.

Maybe, I thought as I dialed, I could just give them a report by phone and that would be the end of it.

My call was answered by a woman, for which I was grateful. She wanted to know my phone number and address, and made sure I was safe. Her voice was terribly even and she asked questions with a completely uninflected tone—no emotional coloring to it.

"You say this was an attempted rape. By this do you mean that the man assaulted you but there was no sexual contact?"

"Yes, that's right." Lord! She might as well have been asking if I wanted chocolate or vanilla.

"And do you know why he ceased his attack?"

"I pushed him out of the car and then I hit him with my flashlight. After that he ran away." It sounded unbelievably simple.

"When did this happen?"

I took a minute to think. The march had been scheduled to start at seven. It was probably about eight, maybe a little after, when I left and started for the car. "Between eight and nine," I said. "I think."

A silence. I looked at the clock; it was now 10:30.

She sighed—the first indication she was anything but an automaton. "Can you establish the time any more closely than that?"

"No, I'm afraid not." I wondered if she thought I'd been drinking.

It turned out she wanted to know the time because a physical examination had to be made within one hour if the report came in quickly enough—even though it was an attempted rape. And she still tried to persuade me to go to the emergency room at the University of California Med Center to have an examination.

"There's no way I'd do that," I told her. "I'm home now, safe and sound. Why should I go over to that neighborhood at this time of night?"

"We can provide an escort. In any case, we will need to send a uniformed officer to your home to interview you."

"What! Tonight?"

"Probably." For the first time she sounded hesitant. "I'm afraid we're having a busy night, I can't say how soon."

This was ridiculous. I wanted to go to sleep. I told her so.

"We have procedures that must be followed. Ma'am, you have been the victim of a felony."

A *felony!* I couldn't believe it. I wanted to just give them a report by phone, and have that be the end of it.

We went back and forth about what I was supposed to do. I learned that I was not obliged to have a physical examination if more than an hour had elapsed; I promised to save my clothes, but announced my intention of taking a shower. And I was able to persuade the police operator not to send a squad car around. Ridiculous! I should stay awake until they were able to come? And then wake up half the neighborhood with the noise and lights in my driveway?

She agreed finally that tomorrow was soon enough to send a uniformed officer to take a report.

After I hung up the phone I must have sat there for a full minute holding it in my hand. A *felony*. And tomorrow a squad car would be pulling into the driveway, in full view of Frannie and the entire neighborhood—Velma Patterson in particular. I squeezed my eyes shut in a futile effort to squeeze the whole thing out of my mind.

I was so tired, overwhelmingly tired. *Bummed* out, I thought—pun intended.

The phone's message light still blinked insistently. I was tempted to drape something over it—hide it so I wouldn't have to contend with it until tomorrow. Instead I reached over and pushed PLAY MESSAGES.

"Emma, I'm so sorry I missed you after the march." It was Brenda Friedman. I struggled to quell my annoyance at the practiced sincerity of her voice.

"Emma . . . I. . . ." The usual assurance was faltering. She started over. "I'm getting more worried about toad man. I've just listened to a phone message left on the recorder at the office. I'm sure it was the same man who sent the dead toads. It has to be. He went on and on, talking about *flattening* us. He sounded as if he were high on something, he was giggling a lot. He'd use a bulldozer to flatten us, he said, or maybe a steamroller. He was damn specific about what we'd look like afterwards."

There was a silence. When Brenda spoke again her voice was brusque.

"Anyhow, we're going to have a meeting about this, and about that strange letter, tomorrow morning. At least, I think so—I've been able to get in touch with almost everyone to set up the session. I hope you can be there. Call me before 10 A.M., will you?"

$\triangledown$

6

I WAS COMPLETELY ZONKED when the phone rang the next morning. I grabbed my little alarm clock and held it close to see the numbers. Eight o'clock. It had to be Frannie. What would she think if she figured out I hadn't been awake? There was no way I could get out of answering—she'd be up my stairs and at my door in a flash.

"Hello," I croaked.

"Good morning, Emma," Frannie said brightly. "I just wanted to ask about that march last night. Was it interesting?"

Interesting . . . not the word to describe last night. I couldn't think of anything to say. My mind was still clogged with the residue of vague, frightening dreams, nightmares in which I was somewhere I wasn't supposed to be, doing something I wasn't supposed to do. I was helpless—being pursued, cornered, trapped. I couldn't move my legs, couldn't scream for help.

"Anyhow," Frannie said, ignoring my silence, "I called to find out if you would—isn't your answering machine working?"

"It's just fine," I said. By this time I'd walked over to the kitchen window to look out. Frannie was up and about ahead of schedule this morning. The curtains by her breakfast nook were already pulled back.

"I left a message," Frannie said. "Is your light blinking?"

"Un-huh." A lie. "I must have missed it last night." Another lie.

"You've been busy, I suppose," Frannie said. Her tone clearly indicated I was remiss, that her feelings were hurt.

As always, I wasn't about to put up with that kind of stuff.

"Look," I said, "you said you called to find out if I would . . . you didn't say what."

"Gracious—yes!" She switched gears instantly. "Emma, the nicest man called me last night."

Her voice held a note of delicious excitement. Here we go again! I thought. I wasn't ready for another of Frannie's romances.

Sourpuss emerged from under the bed, his whiskers draggling shreds of dust. He wasn't supposed to stay in overnight; I'd forgotten to put him out. Trailing the phone cord, I picked him up and headed for the door. Frannie was still going on about the man who'd called. But this didn't seem to be a prospective suitor, she was saying something about investments.

". . . a really *wonderful* opportunity! And—I told you, didn't I?—patriotic, too. Don't you think that's a fascinating idea?"

"Um-hum." I nudged Sourpuss out the door with my foot.

"Mr. Mueller—the man who called—is from the Corinthian Foundation. He told me they're the ones who started the whole idea, making investments in a strong America. Profits and patriotism together, he said. Don't you think that sounds good?"

I thought it sounded like a scam. And an outdated one, at that.

"Anyhow," Frannie went on, "I've got some lovely croissants. Wouldn't you like to come down—maybe in about an hour—and have some coffee?"

"Look, Frannie, I—'

"Oh, don't you dare say no! Mr. Mueller sent me the information. It came yesterday by messenger, right away after I'd talked with him on the phone. The Corinthian

Foundation delivery man was wearing a chauffeur's cap and was driving a big gray limousine. I was *so* impressed."

So that's what that business yesterday had been all about.

"But, Emma, I got to thinking. Gracious! I only know him—Mr. Mueller—over the phone. And to tell you the truth I feel a little foolish. You know—I haven't told you about that yet—he called this morning to make sure I got the brochures."

On top of free home delivery? A scam for sure.

"Anyhow, he said he'd just . . . come over. And so now . . ."

She let it hang there. I didn't take the bait.

"Emma, *please*. Just come down. You can look over what he sent . . . and . . ."

"And then stay while he's here?"

"Yes. Emma, I'm probably acting like a silly billy. He's such a charming man, but he really *is* a stranger. And I didn't even *think* before I invited him."

I didn't want to let myself in for a morning of listening to Frannie go on about this scam-artist, but I realized I had to tell her about last night. The police were going to send a uniformed officer to interview me and I could just imagine Frannie's reaction if she looked up and saw a patrol car in our driveway.

"Emma, won't you come on down and have some croissants."

"Okay," I said.

"Good! Mr. Mueller is coming at ten thirty. So come sooner, all right?"

"I'll be down by ten," I said. "I have something I have to tell you, anyway."

I hung up quickly, before Frannie could ask questions.

The house seemed stuffy. I flung all the windows open wide, but I thought there was still a faint, stale odor of gasoline. I took the plastic bag into which I'd stuffed my shirt and slacks last night and set it out on the porch. Then I made a pot of coffee and put it on to perk, all the while thinking about my reactions—all those nightmares.

I supposed it was usual, a post-trauma shock syndrome,

or some such. But why all the guilt feelings? And all this reluctance to tell Frannie—or, for that matter, to call the police? I knew I'd done nothing to feel guilty about, but apparently my subconscious didn't see things the same way. Maybe it wasn't *liberated* yet. Well, my subconscious be damned!

Half an hour later, I was at Frannie's back door.

By now, having to tell Frannie about last night didn't seem so all-fired difficult. Still, I expected I'd have to sit through a lecture. I'd hear about how, in the first place, these *women libber* groups had the wrong idea—they shouldn't break the rules—and, in the second place, I shouldn't have gone on the march because it was not only wrong but dangerous. Of course, in Frannie's opinion, I was never cautious enough. I took too many chances.

Frannie had a standard speech, which she invoked at regular intervals. "Emma, you should find a more *respectable* way to earn money. I don't like it one little bit, the way you go off by yourself to those old houses and who-knows-where. Why, just thinking about it—you being alone in those strange places—gives me the heebie jeebies. I don't understand why you don't let Vince Valenti help you." At this point she usually gave me one of her sidelong matchmaker glances. "Heaven knows, he's offered often enough."

Frannie has never appreciated either my line of work or hard-earned determination to stay single.

I took a deep breath and knocked on her door.

"I'm in the patio room," she called out. "Come on in."

I'd barely opened the door before she was bustling toward me, smiling. "Emma—you're early. How nice!"

Behind Frannie, in her *patio room*, I could see her silver coffee service ensconced on its huge oval tray on a side table. She'd set out her pink linen napkins, too—the flowered ones.

The room used to be a good old-fashioned sun porch, but that was before Frannie called in a decorator. Now she had it done up to the nines, stuffed full of hanging ferns and potted palms. The fern and palm jungle was kept at bay by two white wicker chairs and a matching sofa upholstered in flowered chintz. The center of attraction was a huge glass-topped coffee table. This was Frannie's favorite room for making a good impression on people. Frannie's very big on first impressions.

I took Frannie by the arm and steered her toward the pink flowered sofa. "Sit down," I said.

"Emma . . . ?" She stared at me, but sat obediently. She gestured awkwardly with one hand toward some glossy brochures on the coffee table.

"Frannie . . ." I felt far edgier than I'd expected. I took a deep breath, and then plunged ahead. "Frannie, something really bad has happened to me. I want you to just listen to what I'm going to say until I'm finished."

She didn't say anything, but picked up a ruffled chintz pillow and held it, her fingers absently pleating the edges of the ruffle. Her brown eyes were on mine, luminous and intent.

"Last night, after the Women Take Back the Night march . . . when I got back to the car . . ." Getting the words out was about as easy as marching through molasses. "Frannie—a man attacked me."

She drew her breath in. Her eyes, enormous and dark, registered confusion, then concern.

"It's all right, Frannie. He didn't—I mean, I fought him off."

She sat very still. I waited, anticipating a speech about why I shouldn't have gone on the march.

"You weren't hurt?" she asked in a small voice.

"No."

She was taking this so calmly, I felt almost let down.

"Are you sure you weren't . . . um . . . hurt?"

"No. I fought him off, like I told you."

"Oh, Emma!" Frannie's voice wasn't calm at all this time. She reached up, took my hand, and pulled me down beside her on the couch. "I'm so sorry this happened to you." She put her arms around me, patting, me comforting me, repeatedly giving me little hugs before she finally turned me loose. "Are you *sure* you're all right?" she asked.

"I'm all right." I felt a lot better, in fact, than I had just a few minutes ago.

"Well now, let's look at you." Frannie put her hands on my shoulders, pushing back and making a show of examining me, the way she used to do with her nieces when they were small—her Aunt-Frannie-will-make-it-well bit. Her voice was a bit quivery, but otherwise she was doing the routine exactly as she did with them. "You look fine to me," she said, cocking her head first to one side and then to the other. She looked at me lovingly. "You look just fine."

I felt guilty for having gotten ready for Frannie at her worst. But when the chips are down, it's always the same—that's when Frannie is at her best.

"You're the tops, Frannie!" I said.

We hugged, long and hard. When we finally disconnected, Frannie pushed back for another *inspection*. "You look downright peaked," she said, playful and mock-peevish. "For Heaven's sake, let's have some of that coffee!"

$\bigtriangledown$

7

AFTER I'D FILLED FRANNIE in on the details of what had happened, I told her I wasn't going to stay. "I really should go home now. I'm supposed to be there when the policeman comes to interview me."

She looked crestfallen.

"Look, Frannie," I said. "I've thought things over. You can get by without me actually being here when Mr. Mueller comes."

Her virtue wasn't at risk; by now I was certain that wasn't what Mueller had in mind. Whether he intended to leave her banks accounts intact was another matter, of course. But the danger didn't seem immediate.

"I have an idea, Frannie. You can tell him I said I *might* come down. That ought to work. You'll be safe enough."

She was plainly disappointed.

"You could set out a coffee cup for me, as if I were due to arrive any minute."

She looked away, then tucked her chin downward and pursed her lips. I hadn't yet hit on what she really wanted.

"I'll tell you what. Before I go, let's just take a quick look at one of those brochures."

Bingo!

All smiles now, she whisked our coffee cups off to one

side. She selected one of the brochures, and, with a flourish, put it square in the center of the table. The cover was in full color, featuring a Marine honor guard and an American flag waving against the backdrop of blue sky and fluffy white clouds.

"This one explains the Corinthian Foundation," Frannie said.

"You know I'm no good when it comes to this kind of stuff," I said. "You should ask somebody else. Elmer Tolverson maybe—he really knows his p's and q's when it comes to investments."

I was wasting my breath. Frannie picked up the brochure, and scrunched closer to me on the sofa. "There are some very nice pictures inside of Mr. Mueller," she said. "Here, I'll show you." She was flipping pages. "His first name is Carl," she added, her voice turning sweet and soft.

The brochure had more pictures than text, every patriotic photo cliché imaginable: men in Revolutionary War costume, portraits of Washington and Lincoln, the faces on Mount Rushmore—even the World War II photo of the flag-raising at Iwo Jima. But nothing more recent.

Frannie opened the brochure to the center spread. "There he is!"

Two full pages were plastered with the man's picture— Mueller saluting the flag, Mueller posing with a Marine in full dress uniform, Mueller standing on the lawn of the White House. Mueller ad nauseam.

I studied a close-up, one of those portraits with all the wrinkles airbrushed. The man was handsome, in a rather fleshy, pale-looking way. His face was a smooth oval, his features symmetrical. His eyes had an odd quality, expressionless and flat—shallow-set eyes, I thought. And I noticed a little American flag pin in his suit lapel.

"Look!" Frannie said, turning to the back cover. "Here he is with his wife. 'Carl Mueller, Corinthian Foundation Director,' it says, 'with Mrs. Mueller.' "

The photo had been taken against what looked like a stage backdrop. It had Greek columns—Corinthian, I supposed.

The Muellers, holding hands and smiling, stood beside yet another American flag. She seemed to be almost as tall as he, but had an aura of elegance. Her coloring was striking—pale skin and dark auburn hair. She wore a ruby-red dress, form fitting but high-necked and long-sleeved.

Frannie sighed. "They're such a nice couple, don't you think?"

"Sure," I said, calculating the odds that the dark auburn hair, done up in a sophisticated chignon, came out of a bottle.

I was beginning to realize that the thing Frannie really wanted was a declaration of approval for the Muellers. There'd be no point in trying to go through the patriotic investment malarky with her, or even in trying to figure out exactly what the Muellers purported to be offering.

"Mr. and Mrs. Mueller look like very nice people," I assured Frannie. I put just the slightest emphasis on *look*—my way of staying honest.

"Do you really think so?"

"They look like nice people," I repeated. "Uh . . . Frannie, I don't know much about financial kinds of things. Before you make any decisions, I think you ought to check with someone like Elmer Tolverson. Or maybe that man down at your bank." But even while I said it, I knew I might as well be talking to the potted palms.

I made my exit as quickly and gracefully as I could, and hurried back up to my place. I *was* supposed to be on hand for the interview with the policeman. I'd also remembered that Brenda had asked me to call her—she'd said before ten o'clock. I was already late.

As it turned out, the lateness of my call didn't matter.

"I still haven't gotten hold of everybody," Brenda told me.

That was odd, I thought. I didn't want to mention it. "I hope you decide to let the police in on this," I said. "I felt pretty useless last night at the march—I mean, as far as being to spot anyone who might have been a threat." I thought a minute, then decided to go ahead and tell her what had happened to me. "As a matter of fact, as it turned out,

I couldn't even see what dangers were out there for myself."

"What do you mean?"

"I was walking alone back to my car. It was right at the time the march ended, and . . ."

"Go on."

I wasn't quite as prepared to talk about this as I thought I'd be. "And . . . this guy tried to rush me just as I was unlocked the car."

"Tried to rush you?"

"Tried to rape me," I said flatly, glad to have it out.

"Are you all right?"

"Sure. I managed to fight him off. I locked myself in the car and drove away." Only it wasn't as easy as I'd made it sound.

"Did you report this to the police?"

"Yes. They're sending someone around to talk to me today."

"What a thing to happen at a Take Back the Night event!"

I didn't want to talk about it. "The point is," I told Brenda, "I don't think Jobs First should rely on amateur protection. I hope you decide at the meeting to call in the police."

"We probably will." There was a peculiar quality to Brenda's voice.

"How come?"

"We really should talk to them now. We've just gotten another letter from our Bible-quoting friend."

8

THE INVESTIGATING OFFICER SENT by the police department came exactly at noontime. Right off, he wanted to
make sure I hadn't actually been raped.

"You're certain there was no penetration?"

He was a young blond giant, soft spoken, and courteous.
He'd asked the question mechanically, as if he asked it often.

"I'm certain," I said, careful to keep my voice expressionless. "No penetration." I wondered if this was all really
routine for him, or if he was trying to be kind to me. He was
writing everything in a large notebook.

"We'll need a physical description."

"Well, he . . . smelled like, I guess, gasoline."

He gave me a look, sharply inquiring. He made a note.

I wanted to explain why I'd mentioned the odor. "The way
he smelled, I thought maybe he'd been living in an old
garage."

The blond giant paused, pencil in mid air. "Ma'am," he
said, very patiently, "we need a physical description. For
example, can you say how tall he might have been?"

"I'm not sure."

Embarrassed at not knowing, I closed my eyes, willing
myself to bring an image of the man into focus. I was careful
to avoid remembering the foul words he'd said, the way he

smelled. I concentrated just on what he'd looked like.

I could remember nothing.

I hadn't been able to see much of him when he'd been on top of me in the car. And when I struggled with him in the street, when I'd had the chance, I just hadn't *seen* him.

"It was pretty dark," I said.

The officer tried to help. He prompted me: weight, coloring, approximate age. I didn't know. I was feeling more the fool with each passing minute, with every question.

"What race was he?"

"White, I guess." Again, I tried to pull together an image. He'd seemed, well . . . *obscure*. Nothing stood out. "I don't think . . . if he'd been really pale, I would have remembered that." Maybe his face was dirty, I thought. Or dark from the sun. "If he wasn't Caucasian, he was pretty close to it," I reported. "Maybe he was Mexican, but I just don't have that impression. No. I don't think he could have been Mexican, or East Indian—nothing like that. He was just sort of ordinary."

"Was his hair covered? Was he wearing some kind of cap?"

"I don't think . . . no, he wasn't wearing a cap." There had been nothing that impressed me about his hair, it must have been sort of *standard*. "His hair was straight, I think, or at least not full-fledged curly. It was fairly dark. Brown, maybe."

"Was he particularly muscular or heavy?"

He couldn't have been, I thought, or I wouldn't have been able to slam him up against the roof of the car. "All I can tell you is that he was probably average size or less, with dark clothes. And he was smelly. He must have been some kind of bum, or close to it."

I'd been an absolute twit, not noticing anything.

My gentle blond interrogator seemed to be satisfied he'd gotten the best description I could offer. He went on to the possibilities for physical evidence, starting with bloodstains.

"Did you strike him during the time you were struggling with him inside the car?"

"No. I just pushed him against the roof."

"Do you think he might have cut himself in any way while you were doing this, or when you ejected him from the car?"

"I don't think so."

"You said you struck him with a flashlight. Do you still have the flashlight?"

"I must have left it in the street. I looked for it in the car and didn't find it." No *bloody* evidence, I thought.

"I'd like to have a look at the car, Ma'am."

We trooped down the stairs. I noticed a large gray Chrysler parked in the porte cochere, the same one as yesterday—not quite limousine size, but close to it. Frannie was entertaining her precious Mr. Mueller.

I opened the garage door. What with the police car parked in full sight and this blond giant and me poking around the Mercedes, I could imagine Frannie maneuvering to keep Mueller from seeing what was going on out in the driveway. No. She wouldn't have to—as long as she had him seated on the sofa in her patio room, he couldn't see out to the driveway. Of course, our neighbor Velma Patterson could. And with both Mueller's car and the police cruiser pulled into the driveway, I expected her to show up any minute.

The officer inspected the Mercedes with great care, even to getting down on his hands and knees and examining the bottom of the car door, and then every bit of the interior. When he was finally satisfied he wasn't going to find anything, we closed the garage door and trooped back up to my place.

I glanced back from the top of the stairs just in time to see the curtain at Velma's kitchen window swing back into place. If I'd spotted her sooner, I'd have given her a cheery wave to let her know she'd been caught in the act.

The policeman was finished with the interview, except to collect last night's clothes from me, and to tell me that I would have to come down to the police department. From the way he said it, this had to be another one of those things he'd said a hundred times. "We'll need photographs of those bruises, Ma'am. Just come down anytime today or tomorrow. Take the elevator up to the fourth floor, I.D. section.

After the photos are taken, you'll be assigned for interview to one of the Sexual Assault and Child Abuse detectives."

He left.

I watched as he walked down the driveway. He opened the trunk of the police car and thrust in the plastic bag with my clothes, then slammed the lid with a casual gesture.

I didn't think they were going to catch the guy who'd attacked me. In fact, I knew it. The gentle blond giant had to know it, too. I couldn't decide whether to be angry about that, or just depressed.

I was still in a rotten mood a little while later when Frannie came up to see me. It didn't help that she was bubbling with enthusiasm about Mueller and his patriotic investment claptrap.

"Emma, he was absolutely *charming!*"

No surprise, I thought.

She was puffing from the climb up my stairs, an excursion she doesn't often take. But every time she's in my place, she makes the most of the opportunity to inspect my housekeeping. I followed her glance around the kitchen. It's not much—vintage stove and refrigerator, and wooden table and two chairs by the window, and over in the corner my rocking chair and one of my grandmother's braided rag rugs. If Frannie had her way, my apartment would be gussied to a fare-thee-well. But this place was built sixty years ago as a chauffeur's apartment; it was meant to be plain. That's exactly how I like it.

Frannie's gaze stopped disapprovingly at the paper bag half full of garbage on the counter, and again at the stack of old newspapers beside my door. Then, seemingly unaware of the time-out she'd taken to survey my premises, she plunged ahead with her account of Mueller's visit.

"We needn't have worried about a thing. He's *such* a gentleman, and he speaks *so* highly of Mrs. Mueller."

I was too out-of-sorts for tact. "Has he asked you yet to plunk down any money?"

I'd hit a sore point.

"Emma, how could you say such a thing! Shame on you!

You never think that I have any sense or that I can—why, only a confidence artist would do a thing like that. Mr. Mueller said so himself."

He was a slick one. He'd come on with a slow windup, I thought, then give her the big pitch.

"You can't be too careful, Frannie. You were talking about being careful yourself, before this character came over to see you."

"Don't you go calling Carl Mueller a character! He's a perfect gentleman." Frannie puffed herself up. "For your information, *Mrs. Suspicious*, he doesn't even have anything to do with the Corinthian Foundation's investment transactions. That's all done directly by the Board of Directors. He just takes care of the education work. That's *his* mission."

And that would be his line of palaver, I thought, word-for-word.

"So what's supposed to happen next?"

"He's making arrangements to present a seminar, which I'll attend," Frannie said sniffily. "The seminar will give me the information I need to choose among the various investment opportunities."

I didn't want to hear any more Mueller-speak. It was time for a quick change of subject. With Frannie, that always works better than arguing the logic of the situation.

"Frannie, don't you want to know how it went when the policeman came up here for the interview?"

"Gracious—such a good looking young man! I saw him going up your stairs."

Frannie listened, genuinely interested, to my recounting of the interview. And she pricked up her ears when I said I'd be assigned to a detective. Only she had it the other way around.

"Just think. A detective assigned to your case."

"Wait a minute, Frannie. What he said was that after I went down and had my bruises photographed, a detective would interview me."

"But with a detective working to solve your case, the police will track down that man in short order. You wait and see."

"Don't get your hopes up."

"Oh, Emma! You're such a glum-pot! How about that gasoline smell for a clue? They could check old garages in that part of town to see if anyone's living in them. Heavens! He might be—"

I'd been over that ground myself, before I thought the situation through.

"Frannie, it's not that simple. Even if they arrest someone as a likely suspect, it probably wouldn't do any good. I don't know what the man looked like. I couldn't pick him out of a lineup, and you can't send someone to jail without a definite, positive identification."

Frannie's enthusiasm faded to dejection. Suddenly she brightened. "Maybe Vince could help," she said.

"Forget it, Frannie."

Vince was the last person I want to see. It was time for another change of subject.

"You know," I said, my voice deliberately casual, "I think the two of us ought to take a look at the Mercedes. There just might be something I missed, and that the policeman missed too—maybe even solid evidence of some sort."

Frannie went for it, much to my relief. "Do you really think so?"

"We won't know unless we go down and see. We can pull the Mercedes out into the driveway—the officer didn't do that. We'll have a good look in full daylight."

$\triangledown$

9

O F COURSE WE DIDN'T find anything.

"I hope they catch him," Frannie said. We'd finished our inspection and were standing in the driveway by the front of the car. "You know, he might even be the Sacramento Stalker."

"The Stalker?" It sounded like a bad joke.

"They were talking about him on last night's news.

"Funny name."

"Umm . . . the police think he's planned his attacks carefully—seems to stake out one territory at a time. First he was somewhere out in Rancho Cordova. Lately he's been in the south area, down the other side of Florin Road."

"How do they know it's the same guy?"

"All the victims reported something about him. The police aren't saying what it is—an identifying characteristic, they call it."

"I wish I knew what it was," I said, thinking of the sudden inquisitive look I'd gotten from the blond giant when I mentioned the gasoline smell.

"Nobody knows. It's supposed to be confidential."

If it was the same man, I thought, he'd switched neighborhoods again. I felt a sudden optimism. Maybe it was the same man. If that smell was what linked him to all the attacks, then someone, out of all those women, must have seen what he looked like. They *would* catch him.

"Frannie, you don't suppose—"

"Yoo hoo! Mrs. Edmundson . . . Mrs. Chizzit!"

Velma Patterson beckoned to us from the gate in her sideyard fence. "I just happened to hear you mention the Sacramento Stalker," she said. She opened the gate and scurried to join us, bringing a garden rake with her. Velma always drags something along—a garden tool, the dog's leash, whatever—to serve as a cover for her snooping.

"It's on that radio talk show right now, about the Stalker, I mean." Velma paused to take a wadded up Kleenex out of the front of her faded housedress. She wiped her brow, then dabbed at a sweaty upper lip. "I was listening to 'Newstalk Fifteen' while I was . . ." She gestured vaguely at the rake. "I couldn't help but notice you two out here." She put the Kleenex back, first giving the perspiration on her bosom a surreptitious swipe. "My, you're real busy for such a hot day—you've had a lot of company, too, I must say."

"What's on the radio about the Stalker?" I asked.

Velma, having secured herself an audience, settled in to her topic. She leaned forward on the rake. "Well, you know, they've brought censorship into it—police censorship."

"Gracious!"

"The police should have stayed out of it, if you want to know what I think. Just because it was the Stalker, that's no excuse to muzzle the nice young reporter who interviewed the co-ed." Velma looked in triumph at each of us in turn, as if to gain ratification for her point. No matter that we weren't exactly following what she had to say—Velma has never been one to squander audience attention with direct, simple discourse. "The reporter meant well, I'm sure," she added.

"I'm sure," Frannie murmured.

"Tell me about the reporter," I said.

"He's from that campus radio station—what's its name? KXPR. He says he didn't know about the police rules." She shook her head. "I don't think they should blame him.

Students aren't supposed to know everything." The wadded-up Kleenex came out again. Velma patted it across her brow, then her upper lip. "I say it doesn't matter whether the reporter knew the rules or not. They shouldn't have rules like that. Where was I? Oh—'Newstalk Fifteen.' They had an editorial first thing this afternoon. And now, what with everybody calling in, they're going to do one of their phone polls."

"They're doing a poll about police censorship?"

Velma favored me with a look that said I wasn't altogether bright. "I told you. The college station broadcast this inter-view . . . let's see, night before last. Yes, that's right, because they broadcast it again yesterday, too. Anyhow, the inter-view was with this co-ed who was a victim of the Sacramento Stalker. The police says she talked about things—details about the rapist—that weren't supposed to get out."

"Did the police say these details were identifying charac-teristics?"

"Something like that. I guess so."

"Goodness!"

"What did the girl who was interviewed say about these identifying characteristics?"

"How should I know," Velma said impatiently. "I never listen to that KXPR station." She scowled at me. "You made me lose my train of thought. Oh, yes. The thing is, the people at 'Newstalk Fifteen' said everybody should have the confi-dential details, not just the people who happened to be listening to that one station. That's the point, don't you think? People have a right, for their own protection."

"Is that what the poll is about?"

"Well of course! They're going to see if the regular news stations—television too—should tell what she said. If the poll says so, they all will. Tonight."

$\triangledown$

1 0

THE TIME BETWEEN NOW and tonight yawned like a great canyon. But the Stalker's identifying characteristic would turn out to be the way he smelled, I was sure of it.

I sat at my little kitchen table with a cup of coffee, staring out my window, and trying to determine how best to use the afternoon. For starters, I decided, I'd check to see if Brenda had scheduled a meeting yet. I was about to make the call when I saw a new-looking Ford Taurus glide into Frannie's porte cochere.

The Taurus was champagne colored. A woman was driving it, I could see her through the windshield. I watched as she reached over to the passenger seat to pick up a briefcase, then held it in her lap, sorting through it. A sales type for sure—what was Frannie getting into now?

The woman opened the car door. She swung out her legs first, keeping her knees discreetly together. Even at this time of year she was wearing nylons and closed, high-heeled pumps. Her ivory-colored suit had a slender skirt. With it she wore a deep reddish-brown blouse. V-necked and tightly fitting. Having gotten out of the car with the grace and poise of a professional model, she stood up. I recognized at once the auburn hair done up in an elegant chignon—Carl Mueller's wife.

She headed for Frannie's side door, briefcase in hand.
Frannie must have been expecting her. She appeared at the
door, opening it wide, and ushered the woman in with her
best pleased-to-meet- you manner.

I had little time to wonder what angle *Madame Chignon*
was pursuing. My phone rang.

"Is this Emma Chizzit?" A woman's voice.

"Yes."

"This is Anne Krouse, from Jobs First."

She was the one with the angry-colored clothes and the
gloomy outlook. Apparently, she didn't remember me from
last night, or at least she didn't remember my name. Brenda
must have gotten around to scheduling a meeting, I figured.
I wondered why Brenda hadn't made the call herself.

"I'm glad to have caught you at home," Annie said. Her
voice sounded a little strange—mechanical, I thought. "We
have so many phone calls to make. Brenda Friedman has
asked us to call everyone."

What now?

"I'm sorry to be bringing you bad news . . ." For a minute
she stopped, not saying anything. Her voice had become
ragged. "Maybe you've already heard . . . on the radio . . .
about Esther Vajic."

"I haven't been listening to the news. I've—"

She interrupted me, speaking quite rapidly now. "Then
I'm sorry to be the one to break this to you—very bad news.
Esther was killed last night. The police found her at her
apartment this morning."

I was too stunned to say anything. Anne continued in the
same rapid-fire style.

"We'll have—there'll be a tape recorded message at the
Jobs First number later, about the memorial service we're
planning to schedule. Please call."

She hung up, and I stood, stunned, looking out the
kitchen window.

I'll flatten you, the toad man had said when he phoned.
And then there had been the letter . . . *to the harlots*. I closed
my eyes, trying to remember the exact words—something

about smashing us to pieces like pottery. And something more. *Now* we would realize.

Maybe we'd received the letter sooner than intended. Maybe *now* was supposed to mean once we knew that one of us had been killed.

$\triangledown$

1 1

I WAS STILL STANDING, staring out my kitchen window, when I saw a dark dusty old Chevy hesitate at the curb and then pull into the driveway. It was, unmistakably, a de-commissioned police car. Vince Valenti's.

Thanks a heap, Frannie. She had to have summoned Old Lonely—why else would he have come?

Vince emerged from his car wearing his police uniform. As always, the polyester blue uniform fit his stout torso badly—the shirt too tight around the armpits and too short to stay tucked in, the pants riding low under his belly. The day had scarcely started to get warm, but already great circles of sweat showed under his arms.

Vince is a huge man, long in the body and short in the arms and legs. He once played semi-pro football, but now he's a policeman in Fairville, a small town about fifty miles west of Sacramento. As nearly as I understand the situation, the Fairville Police Department is eagerly counting the days until he reaches mandatory retirement age. He means well, but he's an absolute klutz.

No matter how many times I manage to avoid Vince, or send him away, or discourage him somehow, he always turns up again sooner or later—usually summoned by Frannie Edmundson, World Class Matchmaker. It's hard to make him understand the words *go away.* Yet when I manage to shuffle him off, I always feel guilty for hurting his feelings.

Vince hurried past the porte cochere and the champagne-colored Taurus, affording the car only a cursory glance, and began stumping up my stairs.

Resigned to my fate, I opened the door as he neared the landing—his blue eyes eager, his face moist. His sparse pale hair was damp, freshly slicked back. Already cowlicks were escaping.

He grabbed me by both arms, gazing right into my face. "Are you all right, Emma?"

"Of course, I'm all right," I snapped, more annoyed with him than I should have been. I broke loose from his ham-fisted grasp and ushered him inside.

"The guy didn't . . . ah . . ." Vince was blushing.

"If Frannie told you what happened, you already know the guy didn't get to me."

Vince looked down at the floor, then out the window. "Um . . . yeah." He turned pleading eyes back to me. "He didn't hit you or anything?"

"He pulled my hair," I said, careful to keep my voice calm and matter-of-fact. "And I've got some bruises on my legs from when he first pushed me into the car."

"Jeez!"

I was sorry I'd mentioned it. He looked ready to explode.

"Come on, Vince," I said. "I'll fix you some coffee."

I told him the whole story, not neglecting to mention the threats that had convinced me to go on the Take Back the Night march in the first place. I didn't think Vince would take to the idea of me having been on the march otherwise, but he's pretty keen on protecting the underdog.

"So they been threatened—the Jobs First ladies."

"By mail, by phone, and by personal delivery."

"Jeez! Dead toads. And that letter with Bible stuff in it."

"That's not all," I said grimly.

He looked up, quick to recognize the changed tone in my voice. "What's wrong, Emma?"

I felt uneasy, I should have told him sooner. "Just before

you came, I got a phone call from the Jobs First office."

He leaned forward, self-consciously touching me on one arm to show his sympathy. "Yeah?"

"Somebody got killed last night."

"Oh, jeez."

"Her name is . . . was . . . Esther Vajic."

Vince pulled his notebook from his shirt pocket and started scribbling—force of habit, I supposed. "Esther," he repeated. "E-S-T-H-E-R. How do you spell that last name?"

"V-A-J-I-C. But the Sacramento police will take care of this."

"Yeah." His tone of voice implied that wouldn't do a good job of it. "You know any of the details?"

"No," I said. "The woman who called just said that Esther had been killed last night and was found this morning. And that it had been on the radio."

Vince finished scribbling in the notebook, and looked at his watch. "I got to get going pretty quick. Costello said he'd cover the first part of my shift, but I don't want to impose any more than I have to."

"You're going right back to Fairville?"

"I got to."

He'd had an hour's ride over, he'd be another hour going back. And I was willing to bet he jumped in his car the minute Frannie called him. I was more annoyed with her than ever.

"Say, who's handling your case down at the Sacramento P.D?"

"Well, I told my story once but I haven't been assigned to a detective yet."

"A uniform came to your place?"

"This morning. And he said I was to go down and they'd take photographs. After that I'll be assigned to a detective."

"You ain't done that yet?"

"No. I haven't had time."

"You got to go right down there and do that."

"I *will*!"

"Jeez, don't bite my head off. I just want to talk to the guy as soon as I know who it is."

"Okay, Vince. I'm going over to the Jobs First office this afternoon, but I'll go by the police station first."

"Promise?" Old Lonely was leaning close, his eager blue eyes searching my face.

"I promise."

When he left, I breathed a sigh of relief. Loyalty, I decided, was Vince's worst trait.

I'd made up my mind earlier to go down to the Jobs First office to see what I could do to help, and take some flowers from the garden. There were some beautiful Gerbera daisies out in that sunny spot by the back fence—in prime bloom, deep reds, and yellows. And, out front, bordering the steps to Frannie's porch, was a whole row of white chrysanthemums. I've never seen the situation that couldn't be improved with a nice bouquet of home-grown flowers.

By the time I'd collected the flowers, Madame Chignon had left.

I went to Frannie's; I'd have to borrow her car again.

Frannie, fresh from whatever sales pitch Mueller's wife had just handed her, reacted badly to the news of Esther's death. At first, she was just as shocked as I had been. After a while, however, it started coming out.

"Emma, it's all because of that march last night." She looked at me reproachfully. "You shouldn't have gone. I shouldn't have let you go."

Let me go. I started to take exception to that, but Frannie turned her back to me and walked over to the breakfast nook in the opposite corner of her kitchen, where the remains of her lunch were still on the table—along with one of Mueller's brochures. She reached out and touched the brochure, as if for moral support. "Marches like that—they're all wrong, you know."

"No, I don't know."

Frannie looked up at me. "Women can be effective in so many quiet ways," she intoned.

The last thing I wanted was a rehash of what Madame

Chignon had undoubtedly had to say on the topic.

"By the way," I said, resorting again to a change of subject. "I'd just as soon you hadn't called Vince. I don't need protecting—and it's not fair to him."

"You hush about that," Frannie said, switching to a light tone. "You do so need protecting."

"It's not fair to Vince," I reiterated. "I'm serious about that. He drove all the way over here just to make sure I was okay."

"Vince can do as he pleases," she said airily.

I gave up and moved toward the utility porch, where Frannie keeps the loaner keys to her car. "We can talk about it later, Frannie," I said. I sighed, deliberately sounding weary. I hate to manipulate Frannie, but it's better than getting into an argument with her. "Can I borrow your car? I have to go to the police station, and I want to go over to the Jobs First office."

Frannie shrugged. "Take the car."

"Thank you."

I left. I should have stayed and smoothed things over a bit, but I was afraid that we might get into it—if not over the garbage the Muellers were feeding her, then over her phoning Vince. No matter, I thought. She was on the defensive about that, so maybe I'd made my point.

Five minutes later I was driving across town, the bouquet of daisies and 'mums on the seat beside me.

My first stop was the police station.

I presented myself at the fourth floor, as instructed. I had a short wait, and then a bored-looking photographer took pictures of the bruises on my legs. I didn't talk to a detective; there were none available. Under any other circumstances, I would have been bothered—I wanted to do everything I could to get that man caught—but I was too eager to get to the Jobs First office.

I was able to get a place to park directly in front of the storefront office on J Street. In the window was a neatly lettered tagboard sign: Women's Job Action Center. The writing was green, in flowing printscript on white tagboard, and outlined with a border of the same green. The sign was flanked by two spectacular Boston ferns in hanging pots.

I peered through the glass front door. It was obvious they were newly moved in—the reception counter was empty of everything except a ring-for-service bell.

There was no one in the front office area, but someone was moving around in the back. I called out an *Anybody here?* and shouldered my way past a curtain strung across the door.

It was Brenda, but not the public persona *grandmother*, lace-collared and demure. She wore jeans and a faded shirt, her Katharine Hepburn topknot hung in a shapeless blob at the back of her neck.

I presented the bouquet.

She gave me a weary grin. "The flowers are beautiful. Anne," she called out. "Come and see. Emma's brought some flowers." She began rummaging through the cupboard by the sink. "I know there's a vase around here somewhere," she said.

I studied the room. One wall was covered with shelves, newly installed, stocked with office supplies and stacks of flyers and leaflets. By the other wall was a computer hooked up to a printer. Beside it stood an old-fashioned Addressograph machine and a number of shoeboxes full of address plates. Along the back wall was a sink and drainboard—kitchen cupboards above and an ancient refrigerator alongside.

Brenda picked up an ashtray from the drainboard. She wiped the contents into a wastebasket by the back door and stepped outside, holding the door open.

"Anne?"

"I'm just emptying this box," Anne answered. A moment later she came in. "That's the last of it," she said, using one arm to brush back a wisp of strawberry blonde hair. Like Brenda, she wore faded jeans—with them a camp shirt, short sleeved, in an ugly plaid, a combination of mustard, green and black.

"I was very sorry to learn about Esther," I said. "It was a real shock."

"Right," Brenda said tersely.

Anne looked away, bit her lower lip.

Brenda gestured with the hand that still held the ashtray, indicating the flowers on the drainboard. "I was looking for a vase," she said to Anne.

But Anne, still struggling with her composure, didn't look at either of us.

I spotted a small plastic wastebasket on the floor in a far corner, and went over to pick it up. "Maybe the flowers can go in here. At least for now."

I wanted to ask about the details of Esther's death, but that would have to wait. I went to the sink for water, got the flowers more or less arranged. "Do you want them in the front window? Maybe under the sign?"

Brenda, busy lighting a cigarette, nodded wordlessly.

I centered the bouquet carefully under the green and white sign. When I came back, Anne still looked jittery, but Brenda seemed more composed.

"Brenda, did you tell the police about toad man?"

"I did." She flashed me a quick grin. "They're now the proud possessors of a box of squashed toads."

"You gave them the letter from our Bible-quoting friend, too?"

She nodded.

"Did you keep a copy? I wouldn't mind having a look at it."

"Kitty made copies," Anne said. Her voice sounded constrained. She cleared her throat. "She gave them to me but they're at home right now." She looked guilty, as if by not having them on hand she'd done something wrong.

"That's okay," I said quickly.

Silence.

I was surprised when Brenda came right to the point a moment later.

"Do you suppose toad man killed Esther?" she asked me. "Or do you think it was the religious nut?"

Her voice sounded too light and unconcerned.

"Right now," I said, trying to match her tone, "I don't

think we have any clear-cut top contenders."

Anne stirred restlessly in her chair. Brenda nervously put her cigarette out.

Another silence.

Anne stood up abruptly, announcing that it was time for her to go back to her chores outside. "You know what Kitty says," she flung over her shoulder as she left. "It's always open season on women."

$\triangledown$

12

Brenda sat very quietly, tap-tap-tapping a fresh cigarette on the rim of the ashtray. "I want to ask you a favor," she said after a moment.

"I'll do what I can."

She took a deep drag, then exhaled self-consciously, aiming the smoke away from me. "I'm beginning to get a feeling about toad man." She stubbed out the cigarette, making quick, nervous jabs into the ashtray. "I think he's ready to quit fooling around. He's made up his mind he's going to *get* us."

"For what you do?"

She nodded. "For what we do—or have done."

I considered mentioning the Bible-quoting letter—not that I thought it came from toad man, but because of the part about *now* we would see the error of our ways.

"We're going to have a new rule around this office," Brenda said. "Nobody works here alone." She gestured toward the alley. "Anne wouldn't be out there by herself, if her husband didn't happen to be in the building next door, attending a meeting."

He was probably as useful as I had been at the parade, I thought.

"Emma, I want you to help watch over the office."

I didn't think that would do any good either, but it couldn't do any harm. "Okay," I said. I supposed I could make the time. Of course, it would put me in a situation of working alone. Not that I minded that. I only minded the presumption that I would be impervious to danger.

I took a closer look around the office. A window above the sink was propped open with a stick. To fix it I'd have to take the window frame out and replace a broken sash rope—a full morning's work for me, being I'm no expert at it. And, below the sink, I'd noticed soggy rags tied around the drain pipe. "I could find plenty to do in here," I told Brenda.

She shook her head. "It's a nice offer, and it would be wonderful to have those things fixed. But that's not what I had in mind. Actually, it might be better if you were just sort of *around*. You could work outside, in the alley maybe."

I doubted that would do any good. But it seemed wiser to me to keep silent and let Brenda and the others have the reassurance. I doubted I'd be in any danger. I'd be coming and going, I told myself, not a sitting duck in the office. I pushed back the thought that I hadn't exactly been a sitting duck when that man attacked me.

"Sure," I said to Brenda. "I'll do it."

The next job I'd contracted for was in this neighborhood, starting Tuesday. I could mosey over from time to time—eat my lunch sitting in the truck out in the alley, or maybe even fuss with something under the hood.

"I'd sure like to find out if somebody is lurking around," Brenda said.

"Got any idea who it might be?"

Brenda's face stiffened into a new expression, totally bland. "No," she said quickly. "There are details about the case the police have asked me not to discuss," she added stiffly.

I wondered what kind of details.

The phone rang. Brenda hesitated, then slowly reached for it.

"Want me to get it?"

She nodded.

"Jobs First," I said, as though I answered their phone every day.

The voice was harsh, guttural. "Bitches . . ."

I signaled to Brenda. "Toad man," I mouthed.

"Bitches," he said again, dragging the word out. His voice grated. Brenda crowded close, trying to share the receiver.

What kind of man made phone calls like this?

"Stay home, bitches," the gravelly voice continued, "or get what's coming to you." Abruptly, he giggled. "You want to see a sample?" Another giggle. "Go look at the front of your stupid office."

He hung up. Brenda and I exchanged quick glances, then raced out to the reception area.

Nothing seemed wrong. The front door was closed securely. I looked through the plate glass storefront window. I saw nothing amiss, no one out front.

I walked forward, cautiously opened the door. Something was hanging from the doorknob, tied with a pink ribbon. It swung with the motion of the opening door, then swang back, splattering dark red blobs.

Brenda sucked in her breath.

It was a huge rat, hung by its neck to the doorknob by a bright pink ribbon, its scruffy fur splotched with blood, its belly cut open and the intestines dangling. The blood was fresh, the innards moist and glistening green and gray. The last of the poor creature's blood still dribbled onto the cement.

"Ugh!" Brenda had her hands over her mouth.

I glanced hurriedly up and down the sidewalk. There was no one nearby, no suspicious figure scurrying away.

I looked at Brenda and shrugged.

"Here goes another call to the police," she said.

At that moment, Anne started screaming.

$\triangledown$

1 3

BRENDA AND I DASHED back through the office and out the back door. Anne stood motionless, backed up against a garbage dumpster amid a pile of empty cartons. She'd stopped screaming, but her hands were clamped over her face and her eyes were wide with terror.

When she saw us, she pointed down the alley. "He ran! That way!"

I could see nothing. We were only about three doors from the end of the alley; we weren't going to find whoever it was.

"Anne!" A man's voice, shouting.

I looked up and saw a stocky, ruddy-faced man at the top of a flight of stairs next door. Other men crowded out onto the landing behind him. He shouted Anne's name again, as he hurried down the stairs.

"Is my girl okay?" He shoved Brenda aside to get to Anne. She moved toward him. "Oh, Tony!"

He put his hands on her shoulders, looking into her eyes. "Is my girl okay?" he repeated, giving Anne a little shake.

The other men crowded around, curious. Anne started sobbing. She tried to cling to Tony.

"Stop your crying! My girl doesn't cry." He pushed her away, his hand gripping tightly as he held her at arm's length.

Tears slid down Anne's cheeks; her chest began to heave silently.

"Stop it!" Tony shook her with a sudden viciousness, snapping her head back and forth.

"For God's sake, Tony!" Brenda shouted.

He glared at her, then pasted on a grin. He abruptly let go of Anne's shoulders; at the same time he maneuvered her so that she was beside him and his arm was around her. Anne stood, frozen-faced but no longer crying. Tony had her totally under his control, pressed tightly against him and his hand clenched on her arm.

He glanced briefly at me, and then defiantly back at Brenda.

"That's my girl," Tony said loudly. He turned his attention back to Anne and brought his free hand up to touch her chin, nudging her tear-streaked face upward with his fist. He clenched his hold on her a little tighter. "*My* girl doesn't cry," he said, and glanced around at the circle of men as if soliciting their approval. "*My* girl's not afraid."

His girl, I thought with disgust. His possession—and she wasn't to exhibit any flaws.

His behavior brought to mind my second husband, Ike. Ike turned out to be a real no-good. He didn't look anything like Tony, but he was the same thing underneath—him and his hard-nosed Australian charm. He used to treat me the same way, wanting to make sure I made him look good in front of his *mates*.

I circled around Tony and moved into position beside Anne. He held Anne's arm with a iron grip. His stubby fingers dug in tightly; the soft flesh of her arm whitened from the pressure of his grasp. I fought back the urge to wrench her away from his control.

"Maybe we should all go back inside," I said, keeping my voice as mild as I could.

Brenda went into action, suddenly shifting to a gracious hostess routine.

"Emma, this is Anne's husband, Tony Krouse. Tony, this is Emma Chizzit."

Tony and I shook hands with mutual reluctance. I made it a point to give him a good glare, and to hold his gaze. He had ginger-colored eyes, and a head of tightly curled ginger-colored hair. His outdoorsy complexion, sunburned and with a lot of lines at the corners of his eyes, gave him a deceptively jolly appearance.

Tony started introducing the other men.

"Clarence, Phil, Bobby, Rodger . . ." He went on, first-naming them all. "Chrissake! Where's Harry." He looked around. "Well . . ." His voice was strained, a bit too hearty. "We'd better get back to it." He started up the stairs, the other men straggling behind.

Brenda and I turned our attention to Anne.

"What happened?" I asked.

"I was out here with the cardboard boxes. I had everything unpacked and so I was going to throw them away. I was in the middle of the stack of boxes, right here by the dumpster." She stopped, hunching her shoulders and hugging her arms. "He must have snuck up right behind me. I didn't know he was there—well, yes, I must have. Something made me turn around."

"Did you get a good look at him?" I asked eagerly.

"No, I just saw a dark figure, and then he shoved me. The stack of boxes fell down, and he ran away." She hugged her elbows, shuddering.

"Come on, Anne," Brenda said, putting arm around her. "Let's go inside. We'll get you a nice cold Coke out of the fridge."

"I'll finish here," I said. I started gathering the toppled boxes, in the process moving as close to the next-door stairway as I could. Several of the men still stood on the stairs. I wanted to listen; I had a notion about what kind of meeting Tony and his buddies were attending.

"What about Harry?" one said.

"Aw, you know." A snigger. "Haven't you learned to spot it yet with him? He's had the urge lately—needs to do some more *research*."

"Put the stopper in, you two," Tony hollered down from

the landing above. "Live and let live."

I was right. First-name-only introductions, the lingo, and now that slogan. This was an A.A. meeting, or purported to be one—Ike's kind, the same sort of rotten-apple crowd he used to favor.

Ike would shun a good A.A. group like the plague. Every time we landed in a new town he'd go from meeting to meeting until he'd found his needle in the haystack, the group that specialized in backsliding. "You don't have to worry," he'd always tell me. "I'm working on my problem." Working on it, my *foot*! It took me a long miserable time to catch on.

I went to work on the cartons, and, when I had slammed the last one into the dumpster, went back inside.

Anne and Brenda sat at the work table, Anne hunching over her cold drink, tracing careful patterns on the wet can.

"I've called the police," Brenda said, her voice deliberately casual. "I told them they could have a two-for-one—the dead rat and the disturbance in the alley."

Anne glanced up briefly, then went back to the patterns in the moisture.

"Maybe it isn't two-for-one," I said, after a moment's thought. "It seems to me toad man could have set up the whole thing for the express purpose of giving us a deluxe scare. First, he hangs the rat on our door, then he makes the phone call from somewhere nearby. He dashes back and sneaks up on Anne while we're out there looking at the rat."

Brenda thought about it for a minute. "Maybe," she said, noncommittally.

"I wish we didn't have to tell them about what happened in the alley," Anne said abruptly. She looked altogether miserable.

"We have to tell them," Brenda said.

The silence was awkward. It lengthened. Anne got up, tossed her soft drink can in the wastebasket and sat down again. Brenda took out a pack of cigarettes, then put them away again.

"By the way," I said, groping for something different to

talk about, "you must have things that have to be done. How are you coming on arranging the memorial service for Esther?"

"It's tomorrow night," Brenda said.

"So soon?"

"We didn't want to do it on a week night. Too many out-of-town people wouldn't be able to come."

"Anything I can do to help?"

"If you want," Brenda said, "you could make some of the phone calls. We've got a list."

"I'll be glad to."

Brenda took a clipboard from one of the shelves. "We're hoping for a big turnout. We've got about a hundred people still to be notified. Let's see. Kitty and her friend took these . . . Lois has the entire second page . . . will you take thirty names?"

"Sure."

She took a page from the clipboard. "It's short notice. Don't worry about making more than one call-back. Either you get them in two tries or you don't."

"I'll do the best I can," I said. I took the list, folded it, and put it in my shirt pocket.

Anne looked up, at Brenda and then at me, misery written all over her face. "Tony means well," she blurted. "He really does. It's just that he—"

Brenda cut in swiftly. "You don't have to apologize for Tony."

Anne looked as if she were going to say more, then sank back in her chair. I went over, sat beside her, and put an arm across her shoulders.

"It's not your fault, Anne."

"I shouldn't have cried like that."

"It's not your fault," I repeated. "You can cry if you want. It's a perfectly reasonable reaction in a situation like that."

Anne kept her eyes down, shaking her head, negating what I'd said.

"Besides," I added, "I understand how it can be with someone like Tony."

Tears squeezed out of Anne's eyes. She shook her head

fiercely. Against my better judgment I plunged ahead. "I used to be married to a man who was a lot like Tony," I said gently. Ike really sold it, I thought, that hard-nosed Australian charm. People who hadn't gotten to know him yet always thought he was *such* a pleasant bloke.

"Ike—my ex-husband—used to act as if he were the most confident man in the world. But underneath he was scared. He was particularly scared about how he stood with his buddies."

Anne looked up at me, her red-rimmed eyes offering me her trust. I gave her one of my best reassuring looks, and a little hug. I was in the mother-figure role again, providing a sturdy, knowing shoulder to lean on—it's sort of a white man's burden for older women.

I went on with my explanation. "Ike lived and breathed for what the other men thought of him." Like a kid in the fifth grade, I thought, and he never grew up. "I could tell him he was doing okay, but what *I* said never counted. It was always Ike's *mates* that counted."

Anne kept those trusting eyes on me, eyes that eagerly searched my face as if there were some special wisdom to be learned from my eyebrows, or the shape of my chin. "I couldn't change things with Ike," I said. "Ever."

I glanced over at Brenda, wondering if she knew about Tony's drinking. Her eyes held my gaze for a moment, then she looked away. She knew.

And I knew there was only one solution to this kind of problem: give the bum the heave-ho. I didn't think Anne was ready to hear that.

$\bigtriangledown$

14

WHEN I GOT HOME, there was a message from Frannie on my phone recorder. She had invited me to supper that night, to listen to the newscasts. And her unconcernedly cheery tone made it clear she wanted to call a truce—we wouldn't have an argument on whether I should have gone on the march, or whether she should have called Vince.

I'd had to stay for quite a while at the Jobs First office, until the police had finished asking questions. It was dinner time already. I hurried down my stairs and across the yard to Frannie's back door. I *hallooed*, then let myself in. I could smell the fragrance of cabbage, mingled with tangy spices and garlic.

Frannie peered around the corner of the kitchen doorway, all smiles.

"Gracious! I was afraid you'd be late for the television news." She hurried back into the kitchen. "Isn't this exciting?"

I wasn't excited—at least, not the way Frannie was. But that's how Frannie deals with potentially frightening situations. She gets into this never-never attitude, transforming everything into a game. It makes the scary stuff safe, with no more reality or importance than who made the most money on *Jeopardy*.

"What's for dinner?"

"We're having Polish sausage. And cabbage, steamed. With carrots and creamed potatoes." She lifted a pot lid, releasing a cloud of cabbage-scented steam. "What happened when you went to the police department?" she asked eagerly.

"I got my bruises photographed. In color."

"And then you talked to the detective?"

"Nope."

"For Heaven's sake! Why not?"

"All the detectives were busy."

She scowled.

"It *is* Saturday, Frannie, not a regular working day. And they told me I'd get a call soon.

"You'd think," Frannie said huffily, "with a case this important, the Stalker and all . . ."

"You're jumping the gun, Frannie. We don't know that the man who attacked me is the Stalker."

On that point, I was deliberately not getting my hopes up.

Frannie turned to me, putting her hands on her hips. "Well *I* think it's the Stalker." Her eyes gleamed. "Just you wait. I'm right. You'll see, we'll hear it on the news—that gasoline smell *is* the identifying characteristic."

She turned back to stir the white sauce.

I kept my silence. There's no point in arguing with Frannie when she's got her enthusiasm up.

"Come on into the den," she said. "I've got our TV trays all ready." She plumped a pillow and indicated where I should sit. "*Now* we'll find out about those identifying characteristics. Turn on the television." She bustled toward the kitchen, then turned back. "Do you want mustard on your sausage?"

"Yes, please."

I clicked on the television.

". . . agreed that information on the Sacramento Stalker would be revealed. We'll have that audio tape when our coverage on this fast-breaking story continues."

A commercial came on. I clicked the sound down.

"It's coming on in just a minute," I called to Frannie. "The announcer said they're going to tell."

"I just *knew* it! Oh—did you say mustard?"

"Yes."

Frannie came in with our plates. The commercial break ended and I turned the sound back up.

". . . revealed by Jonathan Lee, reporter for campus radio station KXPR. In keeping with an agreement made earlier today among news media representatives, we now bring you that audio tape, first aired two days ago. As many of our listeners know, the man described on this tape as the Sacramento Stalker is being sought for the assault of a state college student and a number of other women. And, as many of our listeners also know, the tape contains a passage describing the rapist's *identifying characteristic*. And now, ladies and gentlemen, we re-broadcast the KXPR interview in the interest of public safety."

"Hypocrite," I muttered. "In the interest of ratings is more like it." Frannie shushed me.

The newscaster assumed a posture of intent listening. I noticed that behind him was a map of Sacramento with circles drawn on it, and a blinking light.

The tape started. The woman sounded very young. She spoke in a frightened whisper, beginning her narrative by describing the laundry room and parking lot of the apartment complex where she lived in Rancho Cordova. I turned my attention to the map behind the television announcer. One circle showed the Rancho Cordova area; another a section of the south area, presumably where the rapist had been active. There was also a third area circled—downtown.

I nudged Frannie. "Look! The third circle. That must mean he changed territory."

"Ooooh! We were right!"

A light blinked in the downtown circle, indicating, I supposed, that this was now the rapist's active territory. I turned my attention back to the frightened, whispering voice on the tape.

"I was in the laundry room behind our apartments. He came up behind me. I had no warning, nothing. He just . . . grabbed me, and . . ."

Silence. Then a man's voice—Jonathan Lee, the reporter, I supposed. "Continue when you are ready," he said smoothly.

"He grabbed me. I struggled with him. He pulled my hair."

Just what the man who came after me had done—I listened with mounting excitement.

"He was . . . calling me names, terrible names. Then . . ."

By this time both Frannie and I were leaning forward, straining to hear.

"That's when he . . ."

The reporter's voice interceded. "Do you mean he was successful in the rape attempt?"

I didn't like his tone of voice—the sympathy seemed plastered-on, synthetic.

"Yes," the woman whispered.

More silence. The light on the screen blinked and blinked.

The girl on the tape choked back a sob. "I . . . he dragged me outside. I was so frightened. It was dark—but his hands, I saw his hands in the light from the open doorway. It didn't look like he washed his hands . . . ever."

"If you can," the reporter said in the same smarmy voice, "tell us how this man can be identified. Please, so that others can know."

"The man was dirty—he smelled. I remember how he smelled."

"Gracious!" Frannie wriggled with excitement.

"Please, in order to protect others from this terrible man, identify for our listeners exactly what this smell was."

"Well . . . I guess . . . like gasoline."

"Did you hear that!" Frannie almost wriggled out of her chair with excitement. "It *was* the Stalker who attacked you!"

The television announcer was talking again. I leaned back, paying little attention. I felt enormously pleased. The man who attacked me *was* the Stalker. And he wasn't going to get away with it. They'd catch him—he'd made too many attacks not to have been clearly seen by one of his victims, not to have left behind some kind of physical evidence.

The announcer was concluding the news broadcast. I

picked up my fork and poked a hole in my Polish sausage, releasing a torrent of fragrant juice. I began cutting the sausage into bite-sized pieces.

"Women are being cautioned to stay off the streets if at all possible," the announcer said. "Fear, already running high in Sacramento neighborhoods haunted by this brutal man, is now at fever pitch."

"I guess that's it," I told Frannie, taking my first forkful of sausage. It was delicious. "Mmmmm," I said, waving my fork at Frannie. "Good."

"We'll be right back," the announcer went on, "with news of measures taken by officials in the wake of strong public reaction to new developments in the Stalker case."

"Gracious! They'll catch him now, don't you think?'

"For the benefit of those who may have tuned in late, we repeat the information revealed at the start of this broadcast," the announcer said. "Police have confirmed rumors circulating earlier. They have information linking the Sacramento Stalker to the death of women's rights activist Esther Vajic."

Frannie gasped.

"We repeat. Police now confirm that activist Esther Vajic was slain last night by the Sacramento Stalker."

I was gasping too, fighting for breath. I pushed back as far as I could in my chair, away from my plate, trying to ignore the heavy smell of the sausage, the sheen of grease glistening on my cabbage. I stared at the far-away-seeming television screen, where a tiny smiling woman tossed laundry into a washing machine.

I tried to tell myself I hadn't heard the announcer say the Stalker killed Esther Vajic. But the chilling truth was there, an icy certainty.

Warmth roiled my stomach; I sat up as straight as I could. I swallowed the saliva gathering in my mouth, and swallowed again. The television set seemed at an even greater distance, but I could still see the tiny woman and her washing machine. I couldn't hear what she was saying.

I put my head back, pulling in long breaths.

The question was inescapable: which one of us had he attacked first?

I resisted thinking about it, told myself there wasn't any answer I could know. But I knew. I'd hit the man. The flashlight had connected solidly with flesh. I'd felt the impact, known. The fight was over in that instant, because I'd disabled him.

"Frannie," I said, astounded at the calmness in my voice. "When he came after me, he'd just killed Esther."

$\triangledown$

15

I MUST HAVE LOOKED like I'd been pole-axed.

Frannie was all over me with ministrations: wanting me to put my feet up, feeling my forehead, dashing to get me a cold cloth, trying to persuade me to put the recliner back to its farthest position. By the time she was headed for the kitchen to get ice cubes and fill her ice bag, I'd already regained my composure.

"Frannie," I called after her. "Relax—I don't need an ice bag, for Pete's sake!"

She stopped halfway through the kitchen door to remonstrate with me. "Don't argue with me, Emma Chizzit. You should have seen yourself. Heavens! You must have turned six shades of green." She proceeded into the kitchen, muttering that I never took care of myself properly.

Rescue came from an unlikely source. From my vantage point in the den I could see out the window; Mueller's big gray Chrysler was gliding to a stop under the porte cochere.

"You've got company," I said.

Frannie peered quickly toward the side door, then let out a startled "Oh, my!" She rushed to the hall mirror to poke at her hair and smooth her dress.

I picked up our trays and started for the kitchen. I intended to make a quick exit out the back door before

Frannie admitted her company. But she was too fast for
me—she'd already opened the door and was escorting the
Muellers into the hall. "Emma," she called, "come and meet
Carl and Rachel."

Carl and Rachel. Worse and worse.

"Gracious, don't fuss with those supper things. Come on
in here—in the patio room."

I was trapped. I presented myself. Mueller got to his feet
immediately. "Ah, Frannie! This must be your friend,
Mrs. . . . ?"

"Chizzit," I said.

"*So* pleased to meet you." His voice dripped automatic
sincerity.

He offered me a professional salesman's firm handshake.
As far as I was concerned, any good impression supposedly
imparted by the firmness of his handshake was negated by
the softness of his skin—most women don't have skin that
soft. There was a softness to him altogether, and, in person,
he had the same pale-flesh look I'd noticed in his picture.
He was clearly someone who'd spent all his life indoors:
never hiked or camped, never chopped wood—never even
gone fishing, probably. Not that he wasn't handsome, or that
he wasn't a *fine figure of a man* in his perfectly tailored dark
suit as he stood by the coffee table, more or less at parade
rest.

Frannie, eager to introduce me to Mueller's wife, was
making little fluttery motions.

"Rachel," she said, "this is Emma Chizzit."

Mueller's wife got up from the sofa to greet me with a lithe
motion, the same professional grace I'd noticed when I'd
watched her get out of her car. I was willing to bet she'd once
worked as a model, though she was no longer model-slender.
She had one of those narrow-hipped figures, with a good set
of shoulders and generous proportions above the waist—the
kind of physique that used to be called *deep chested*. She
wore a plum-colored silk dress, sleekly fitted, and high heeled
shoes in exactly the same color.

She also presented me a softer-than-silk hand. "Mrs.

Chizzit, what a pleasure to be meeting you at last." She kept hold of my hand and leaned forward slightly, gazing directly into my face.

On close inspection I could see that she was wearing a lot more makeup than a person might realize at first glance. Under all that expertly applied paint her skin was parchment-fine, with networks of tiny wrinkles around her eyes. Madame Chignon was no spring chicken—and, I was willing to bet, at least five years older than her husband.

"We've been hearing the nicest things about you," she said to me, and then turned to her husband. "Sweetheart, isn't that so—hasn't Frannie told us what a wonderful friend she has in Emma." Her voice was saccharine.

She was no fool, I thought. She'd already figured out I might throw a monkey wrench into their plans for getting Frannie's money.

"You're absolutely right, Cupcake."

Mueller turned to me. "Our dear Frannie has told us *so* much about you." His voice exuded warmth; his eyes were stony cold. "Any friend of Frannie Edmundson is a friend of ours." He turned to his wife. "Isn't that right, Cupcake?"

Mrs. Mueller crinkled her eyes at the corners, and arranged her lips into a smile.

Frannie was in seventh heaven. "Do sit down," she said, gesturing toward the couch. "I'll just fix us some coffee."

"Oh, please—don't bother," Rachel said. "We're on our way to dinner, we just dropped by to leave some materials with you."

Mueller reached for the briefcase he'd brought with him. "I'm so pleased that you've consented to be a sector captain at our seminar on Sunday night," he said to Frannie.

Sector Captain!

Frannie, settled contentedly in one of the wicker chairs, beamed with delight—entirely sold on this childish malarky.

Rachel sank back smoothly to her seat on the couch. She still had hold of my hand, so I had no choice but to sit beside her. Frannie was getting her marching orders as sector captain; I was trapped into private conversation with Rachel.

She flapped her mascara laden lashes and favored me with another of her so-called smiles. "I'm so glad we have this little chance to talk," she said. She leaned forward and gazed directly into my face as she had before, tapping me on the wrist with her fingertips to claim my attention. "Carl's special realm is his educational mission for patriotic investments." Her voice was low and urgent. "I have my mission, too." She lowered her voice further, leaning closer yet, as if she were about to impart something top-secret. "My mission—a *woman's* mission—is family preservation."

"Is that so?"

She went in for some more eyelash flapping—in discouragement, I hoped.

"Family preservation is *so* important. That's why we all have to pull together, pull together as *women*. We have to *actively* enhance the strength of the family in these troubled times . . . help the American family . . . *protect* the American family."

She was clutching my wrist. Tightly.

"Do you mind?" I extricated it.

"So sorry," she murmured, then smiled brightly. "I *do* get excited when I explain our crusade for the American family."

"Obviously."

I was tired of being polite to Madame Chignon and her oily husband. They were both con artists. I sat immobile, wearing what I hoped was my best stone-faced expression.

Frannie's hostess antennae must have started vibrating. She immediately turned to us. "Gracious!" she said, aiming an encouraging smile at me. "Isn't it wonderful what Rachel does, Emma. Has she been telling you?"

"She hadn't got down to details yet," I said.

Carl Mueller interrupted us. "We really must be going now."

His wife began rummaging in her purse. "Mrs. Chizzit, I've got something *very* special for you. This will tell you *exactly* the steps we're taking to protect the American family from bad influences."

I glanced at the brochure. Another Mueller Special—a full

color picture on the front showed the inevitable flag flying against a blue sky. The red, white and blue was backdrop for a blonde, blue-eyed woman holding a baby. Lettering across the top proclaimed that this was the quarterly magazine of the *Organization for Democracy and the Family*.

"You say you protect the American family from bad influences?" I said to Rachel. I glanced over to Frannie, wanting to make sure she was listening. "Exactly what influences do you think are bad?"

"We have to be constantly on the watch," Rachel said smoothly, "Alert at all times for danger." She turned to her husband. "And we have to warn people, don't we, Sweetheart."

He nodded. Frannie nodded, too.

Rachel moved closer to Frannie, an ill-concealed gleam of victory in her eye. "We screen out evil messages, protect the children. It takes constant monitoring—we keep track of record albums, radio and television programs, motion pictures, bookstores." She was all dignity, making a show of a gallant response in the face of my questioning. "And, of course, we do not limit ourselves to monitoring and providing warnings. In special cases that come to our attention, we provide direct support to deserving families." She turned to Frannie. "I'll be telling you more about that soon," she said.

Frannie nodded eagerly.

"Our most important work," Rachel said.

"Funded entirely by donations," Mueller added. "The only way to assure preservation of our democratic society."

Frannie's head bobbed up and down in vigorous agreement.

Score Round One to the Muellers, I thought.

"We really have to be going," Mueller said, shifting restlessly on his feet.

Rachel leaned forward and sideswiped Frannie's cheek, leaving a smudge of dark red lipstick. "See you at the seminar, dear."

After they'd left, Frannie sank into a chair and sighed.

"They're wonderful people—and such a romantic couple, too. Tonight is their wedding anniversary—Rachel told me so." Another sigh. "I think it's so sweet when couples can keep the romance alive."

"Frannie, I'm tired. Let's talk about the Muellers some other time."

"They really are very nice people," Frannie offered.

I said nothing.

"Carl has such gentlemanly manners, don't you think?" she persisted.

"I suppose so," I said. "Very well dressed," I added, hoping to get off the subject."

Frannie spoke very softly. "You could have been a bit more friendly."

"Frannie, I'm sorry, but I'm tired. I have to go home now. I have a bunch of phone calls to make before I get to bed tonight."

She looked startled. "Phone calls?"

"Yes." I tapped my shirt pocket with the list of names and phone numbers Brenda had given me. "There's to be a memorial service for Esther Vajic tomorrow night. They have a recorded message about it on the Jobs First phone, but they need more outreach than that—we're all taking a share of the phone list."

Frannie scowled. "*Outreach*! Why, Emma, you're talking like one of those activists."

"Sorry, the word just slipped in."

My sarcasm was wasted, Frannie went right on without skipping a beat. "What are they thinking of anyhow, giving you all those phone calls to make. Considering what you went through last night—"

"Consider what *they* are going through, Frannie. Someone they worked with every day has just been murdered."

"Oh!" She looked contrite, irresolute. "Well . . . I still don't think you should be up late making phone calls. Not tonight."

"I only took a small share. The others are making calls too."

"Then, for Heaven's sake . . ." She held out her hand, indicating I should give her the list. "Let *me* make your calls."

I handed the list over and told her what to say. Frannie is nothing if not unpredictably generous. And totally apolitical. Maybe, I thought—without much hope—I could still find a way to back her off from the Muellers and their claptrap nonsense.

I thanked Frannie, hugged her good-night, and started home.

By the time I reached my back door I was smiling. I'd been struck by the look I would see on Mueller's face if he could hear Frannie making the phone calls. *Hello, this is Frannie Edmundson, calling for Jobs First. . . .*

$\triangledown$

16

THE NEXT DAY—SUNDAY—I KEPT to myself the entire morning, enjoying Sourpuss's company and reading the paper. By the time I'd finished lunch, however, I had a full-blown case of cabin fever. I stood on my little front porch, leaning against the railing and considering what to do between now and this evening. Tonight I would drop Frannie at Mueller's seminar, and go on to the memorial service for Esther.

My eye lit on the ivy growing on the back fence—overgrowing would be a better word. Within a minute I had my work gloves out and was in the back yard, going at the ivy with a will.

I worked my way down the fence, wrenching loose long runners and stacking them into piles to cart away later. I got out my hammer and nails, too—from time to time I had to mend sections of fence that pulled loose when I tore away the ivy. I managed to get in an hour or more of good, satisfying work before Frannie appeared.

"Emma! You'll wear yourself out."

By this time I'd gotten out my shovel and was getting after a big piece of ivy root by one of the fence posts. I turned around and straightened. I mopped my brow, then surveyed the piles of ivory runners and pulled-up roots—a ragged row across almost the entire width of the back lawn.

Frannie was looking at the prunings, too. "I had no idea the ivy had gotten so out of hand."

I turned back toward the fence and started digging again. "Don't worry, Frannie, I'll get it all carted off before it's time to get ready for tonight."

"Oh, I wasn't—that wasn't what I came out for. I wanted to ask whether you think my faille suit would be too dressy for tonight. You know, the one with the peplum."

"Sounds fine to me." I kept working.

"Oh, by the way . . . I suppose you're going to wear your gray suit."

I nodded. It's the only thing I have with a skirt.

"You know . . . I think it would be nice if you wore that cranberry-colored blouse with it."

I stood up, propping the shovel carefully against the fence. "I'll be glad to." Frannie was anxious about tonight, I told myself—I shouldn't be annoyed. "I suppose that would go better with something you're planning to wear."

"As a matter of fact . . . my pin with the rubies in it."

I came close to laughing out loud. The Muellers would scarcely see me when I stopped to drop Frannie off—let alone what kind of stones were in her lapel pin. Unless . . .

"Frannie, you're not going to try to talk me into coming to the seminar instead of going to the services for Esther, are you?'

She smiled sweetly, and shook her head.

"Well," I said, "I guess I'd better get started cleaning up this mess."

Frannie's sweet smile persisted.

"Anything else, Frannie?"

"Oh . . . uh . . ." She was up to something, she was giving me one of her sidelong looks. "You haven't heard anything more from Vince, have you?"

"No. Should I have?'

"Well, I don't think so. I just thought he might have found something out and given you a call."

"I haven't heard a thing."

Frannie, apparently satisfied, went trotting back into the house, leaving me to wonder why she'd mentioned Vince. With Frannie, there's no telling.

I began picking up the piles of ivy runners. Before long I noticed one last section of the fence down by the corner that I'd forgotten to nail back into place.

I got the board into position and whacked in a few nails. It needed fastening on the back, too, so I hoisted myself up on the corner post and leaned over on the alley side, trying to determine the best place to position my first nail. I must have been altogether engrossed in what I was doing; I didn't hear a thing until the jogger pounded by, only inches away.

He was breathing hard and pelting along for all he was worth. I caught a glimpse of a beet-red face and pale blue eyes behind wire-rim glasses. Sweat was streaming down his face from his thinning pate. He was pared-down, lean almost to excess, his running shorts flapping against his skinny bottom. His footfalls made little puffs of soft gray dust as he thudded away down the alley, gone in a flash. I shut my eyes, clinging to the fencepost.

The sound of his breathing, so close . . . hard breathing . . . like the man in the front seat of Frannie's car. I clutched the post harder, squeezed my eyes shut tighter still.

He'd just killed Esther. How much earlier? Ten minutes? Half an hour?

There was no point in thinking about it.

I snapped my eyes open to bright sunshine and an empty alley and silence. Disgusted with myself, I clambered back down off the fence. I'd dropped my hammer; I had to go out to the alley to retrieve it.

The man was just an ordinary running freak—why did I have to feel so afraid? More to the point, why did some bum think he had the right to go around raping women . . . killing one?

Maybe the Women Take Back the Night march wasn't such a dumb idea after all.

17

T HAT EVENING I MANAGED to show up a few minutes early at Frannie's, which seemed to please her no end—and also contrived to maintain a tactful silence. Barnum was right, I thought, there's one born every minute; Frannie chattered in happy anticipation of Mueller's seminar, eager to play her role as *sector captain*.

As I threaded the Mercedes through the traffic around the convention center, I tried to think of some way to dampen Frannie's ardor. There seemed little hope, until she mentioned that Mueller was looking for individuals to host follow-up seminars.

"Carl feels that a formal seminar is necessary to launch a program in the community, but then he wants the friendly atmosphere of a private home—someone giving a nice little evening coffee or tea. That's so much nicer, don't you think?"

"Um," I said, faking concentration on the traffic.

"I'm going to ask the Tolversons," Frannie said. I was surprised, I would have expected her to hostess one on her own. "You gave me the idea," Frannie added.

"What?"

"Of course you did. Don't you remember telling me that Elmer really knew his p's and q's when it came to investments?"

This was an interesting development. I couldn't imagine hard-headed Elmer and Elvira Tolverson falling for Mueller's line of malarky.

We approached the entrance to the main hall, and I looked for a convenient spot to pull over to the curb. Things didn't seem right to me—the sidewalk was thronged with young people, not the investment type.

We both saw it at the same time, the banner over the entrance: SKI SWAP AND TRADE FAIR.

"Oh! No! There must be some mistake," Frannie exclaimed in dismay.

"What happened at Mueller's seminar?" I tried not to sound smug—a valiant effort.

"I . . . don't know." Frannie looked around in confusion as we inched forward through the traffic.

"You're sure he meant the convention center?"

"Yes! I suppose—oh, look! The Muellers *are* here. See? There's their car."

Sure enough, their Chrysler had pulled to the curb a few car lengths ahead of us. A man in a chauffeur's suit—the one who'd delivered the brochures—climbed out. He opened the door to the back seat and stood stiffly as Carl Mueller emerged and then made a big show of ushering out his wife. Rachel was dressed all in black, a form fitting V-necked dress, and had added to her chignon a great number of extra swirls and swoops.

"Ooooh—doesn't Rachel look beautiful! I'm so glad I wore my faille suit."

"It looks like the seminar *is* here somewhere at the center," I said. "Aren't there some smaller meeting rooms around to the back." I hadn't been able to avoid putting just the slightest emphasis on *smaller*.

Frannie gave me one of her I'm-ignoring-what-you-just-said looks. "Emma, won't you take time out to at least come and say a friendly hello to the Muellers?"

"Sorry, Frannie. There's no way I'm going to find a place to park."

"Well . . ." She was looking for a parking spot, trying to

verify what I'd said.

"I'm going to have to let you out when we stop for the light at the corner."

"Maybe you can visit with Carl and Rachel afterwards," Frannie said, sounding disconsolate.

"Here's where you get out," I said, and then decided to accommodate Frannie on this if I could—the more open I was in my distaste for these con artists, the less she'd listen to me and the more advantage I'd give them. "Look I'll do the best I can to be back by nine-thirty. Maybe that won't be too late for the Muellers. I'll meet you at the Boulevard Coffee Shop. Okay?"

Frannie agreed, having brightened considerably. She clambered out of the car and hurried toward the convention center.

The memorial service for Esther was being held at the St. Francis Catholic Church social hall, only a few blocks farther down J Street than the Jobs First headquarters. As I drove toward it, I fought a tug-of-war with my conscience over how hard I'd try to be back at nine-thirty.

I was startled when, up ahead, near the Jobs First office, I saw flashing lights—police cars! Two black and white units were parked in front of the office; people milled in the street. I drove slowly past, waved onward by an impatient-looking policeman.

Words were spray-painted on the front of the building: STUPID BITCHES.

Toad man, I thought, noticing at the same time that the front door stood open at a crazy angle, wrenched loose from its top hinge.

I turned at the corner, found a place to park, and came back. As I walked up to the crowd in front of the office I could see Brenda talking to the police. Kitty Hackett stood nearby.

"What happened?" I asked Kitty.

"Some guy was just here doing this. Can you imagine? The people across the street saw him and called the police."

I peered inside the storefront window. The place was a mess: dirt from the fern pots all across the floor of the reception room, a literature rack tipped onto the floor, leaflets strewn everywhere. I didn't want to think what havoc he might have created in the back room.

"Toad man?" I asked Kitty.

"I'd bet on it."

"The police didn't catch him?"

"No. He'd gone by the time they got here. But at least we got a description from the people across the street, they're the ones who phoned the police. They said he was a swarthy man, dark haired. He had a beaky nose, and he was in coveralls—bare-chested underneath with a mat of hair showing."

After that we waited in silence, listening to the unintelligible crackling of the police car radios. Finally Brenda ceased talking with the officers and came over.

"Well?" Kitty said expectantly.

"They think they know who it is."

"Who?"

"Someone we've known all along—and never thought of." Brenda gave us a wry smile. "A well-known troublemaker, Benny Podesta. They've put out a bulletin on him."

"Him!" Kitty exclaimed. She turned to me. "A macho nut. He's the one they arrested for showing up in a dump truck and trying to chase away the television reporters when we did the construction site demonstration."

$\triangledown$

1 8

Esther Vajic Memorial signs at the front of St. Francis Church directed people around the side to a large courtyard. The courtyard was nearly empty; a last few about-to-go-inside folks lingered by the social hall entrance.

I started in.

"Emma! Emma, wait for me!"

I turned. It was Anne. She hurried across the courtyard.

We started in to the hall, but a young man, one of the ones who had been standing by the entrance, put out a hand to detain us. He had a clean-cut look about him, a slender build and rather Nordic features; light brown hair spilled lankly across his forehead. He was dressed preppie-style—khaki pants and a Madras shirt, a lightweight sweater tied carelessly across his shoulders.

"You must be Emma Chizzit," he said to me, flashing an ingratiating smile. He ran a hand through his hair to smooth it back from his forehead before he offered to shake hands. "Jonathan Lee," he said. "KXPR radio."

The smarmy reporter. "How did you know me?"

He grinned. "Brenda Friedman didn't have time to talk to me before the meeting, but she said you'd be coming along soon. Then I heard your friend call your name—there's not

that many Emmas around." He looked at Anne. "And you
are . . . ?"

She gave him only her first name.

"Anne," Lee said smoothly, "weren't you and the other
members of Jobs First terribly frightened when you first
learned of your friend Esther's death?—frightened for your
own safety, I mean."

He had produced a tape recorder and a small notebook,
and now leaned confidently back against the rail of the entry
steps, apparently intending to interview us at some length.

"We don't want to be late for the memorial service," I said,
deliberately brusque. I took Anne by the elbow and propelled
her up the steps. Lee trailed behind.

The main room of the social hall was rather large, and also
low-ceilinged. There was a stage at one end, the sort of
glorified platform that used to be common in elementary
school auditoriums. Brenda and Kitty were seated there on
folding chairs, along with Coretta Vajic, Lois Muldoon, and
some people I didn't know. My eye was immediately drawn
to a spot at the right of the stage, where my chrysanthemums
and Gerbera daisies were on display in a large deep-yellow
vase. They looked every bit as good as I'd expected they would.

Anne and I took what seemed to be the last two vacant
sets, at one end of the very back row. Lee, undaunted, found
a folding chair and brought it over to sit near us.

He leaned forward, his notebook at the ready. "Tell me,
Anne, who are the people up on the platform?"

"Why are you here?" I interrupted.

He smiled ingenuously, putting a lot of boyish charm into
it. "Mrs. Chizzit, there was a recorded message at the Jobs
First number, which I called after I learned of Esther Vajic's
death."

"But why did you call the office?"

Another grin. "I'm a reporter. I'm researching a series on
violence against women—which happens to be a very hot
topic right now. Satisfied?"

Hot topic. My hackles rose. That's all we were to him—a
means to achieve his ambitions.

Lee shifted his attention back to Anne. "Tell me about those folks up on the platform, Anne."

She didn't seem to notice to condescension, and began naming the people seated on the stage. "That's Brenda Friedman, you know who she is," Anne said. "On her left are Lois Muldoon and Coretta Vajic, two of our board members."

"And Mrs. Vajic is, of course, Esther Vajic's mother."

"Yes."

"Is someone supposed to be seated in the empty chair on the other side of Brenda Friedman?"

Anne blushed. "Me."

"You're a board member, too?"

"Yes."

She'd spoken reluctantly. "I'm new on the board."

Lee leaned toward her. "Anne, do you want to tell me your last name?"

"Krouse." She spelled it for him.

"Good girl!"

My ire grew.

"Now, Anne, what about the people in the second row?'

"That man at the end is Al Friedman, Brenda's husband."

It hadn't occurred to me that Brenda might be married—the man would have to have the patience of a saint. I hadn't noticed him before, a skinny man in a tan corduroy jacket and glasses. Wire-rim glasses.

He was the jogger I'd seen this afternoon! His hair was neatly combed and his face, now that it wasn't red from running, was rather pale. But it was him, no mistake.

"Al Friedman's a professor over at the university," Anne said. "Geology." She sighed. "He's just a wonderful man!"

Anyone's husband, I thought, would look good to Anne in comparison to Tony.

"Geology department?" Lee's voice was suddenly sharp. "Wasn't he the one who had to take the heat for that Carmen Cassidy flap?"

Anne looked puzzled.

Carmen Cassidy, Junior: young, black and female—also

pushy. I'd seen her interviewed on television in the midst of all that controversy. A real pistol. She wiggled her body when she talked, and smiled boldly into the television camera. "My Mama told me I was Carmen Cassidy, *Junior*, and I should never forget it!" She'd made a good case for her stand that she was the best candidate for a position that was open in the geology department. Those must have been troubled times in the Friedman household—Jobs First had taken up Carmen's cause, blocked traffic and all the rest.

Brenda got up to speak; the room became suddenly silent.

Lee started to ask Anne another question. A woman beside me angrily shushed him, gesturing toward Brenda. I was impressed with Brenda's poise—that she could seem so calm in the face of the mess Benny Podesta had just made of the office. She was talking about her memories of working with Esther, but mostly about the goals Esther wanted to achieve. Jonathan Lee, prize reporter, wasn't taking notes. This didn't have enough of the damsel-in-distress flavor to be his kind of stuff, I supposed.

Brenda reviewed Esther's career, then began talking about a project that she'd had in the works just before her death— an art show based on the theme of women's work and women's achievement. Esther, Brenda told us, had long cherished this project, and had given it a name, Women Working Wonders.

Brenda repeated the name in loud, ringing tones. "Women Working Wonders! We're going to have the art show Esther Vajic wanted, we are going to have Women Working Wonders this very next weekend, right here in Sacramento!"

The audience buzzed with surprise, then clapped and cheered. Putting together something like that on such short notice sounded impossible to me. I turned to Anne. "How on earth . . . ?"

"Brenda's already got it started," Anne whispered. "There's a collection of Dorothea Lange photographs over at the University of California Davis campus—the Women's Studies people over there owe us a favor and will loan it. Then Lois will work with the schools. The idea is to have kids bring in captioned photos of their moms at work, and lifesize cutouts showing themselves in the careers they want to have. And Kitty will—"*

"Shhh!" Our neighbor flashed us an angry look. Brenda was still speaking.

"We want creative expressions from everybody. All of us must help bring them in. Organizations, people of all ages, school children, volunteer groups, art and photography students, parents—senior citizens, too." She was looking right at me.

I noticed that several women from the back of the room had come forward. They began distributing flyers and taking up a collection.

Anne nudged me. "Brenda's idea. She said people would want to donate money in Esther's memory."

"Mrs. Chizzit," Jonathan Lee said, putting on his most ingratiating smile, "I'd like to get back to the story I'm covering. I want your reactions. Tell me, weren't *you* terribly frightened when you heard of Esther Vajic's death at the hands of the Sacramento Stalker?"

If it weren't for my longstanding faith in the principles of non-violence, I would have hit him.

$\triangledown$

1 9

THE NEXT MORNING, MONDAY, I phoned first thing to see how soon I would be able to pick up my truck. The parts for it had just come in, they told me. It would be ready in two hours.

I spread out the *Sacramento Bee* on my kitchen table alongside my breakfast. In the local news section I found a brief item about the memorial service for Esther, but nothing about the office being vandalized. It was just as well—no sense in rewarding the likes of Benny Podesta with publicity.

Frannie had been shocked to hear the news last night. It had been nearly ten o'clock by the time I'd come back to the Boulevard Coffee Shop from the memorial services—too late to be inflicted with the Muellers' company. Frannie was disappointed. I caught a glimpse of her from outside; she sat at a little white plastic table with three coffee cups in front of her, looking altogether forlorn. I'd hurried in, hoping that the office vandalism incident would distract her from the disappointment. She'd refused to be placated. I'd *promised* to be there at nine-thirty, she'd said, pouting.

Well, Frannie would just have to stew in her own juice.

I added the morning's paper to the stack by my door, reminding myself that I'd soon need to embark on a good housecleaning. I poured a second cup of coffee and went to my porch to take in the morning breezes.

Vince's Chevy was parked in the driveway—Frannie's doing, no doubt. She must have called him yesterday after we got home, after his late shift of duty.

Vince was nowhere in sight. I checked Frannie's kitchen curtains. They were still drawn, but it was past eight o'clock so I doubted she was sleeping in—laying low was more like it. I stared in consternation at the closed curtains and the dark, dusty car.

As if on cue, the back door opened. Vince, carrying a small duffel bag, let himself out. He looked up, saw me, and gave an eager wave. He put the duffel bag in his car before he started across the back lawn toward my place.

Resigned, I greeted him at the top of the stairs. "Come on in, Vince," I said. "You want some coffee?"

"Golly, I sure do."

He came in, looked around, and—as always—blushed. He was in my boudoir, unchaperoned.

"Sit down." I gestured to my little kitchen table. "You want some toast, too?"

He nodded. "Frannie called me last night, about that office getting vandalized," he said, fixing me with his earnest blue-eyed stare. "She's real worried about you."

It sounded to me more like World Class Matchmaking in action. "And she invited you to come over and see if you could help."

"Yeah." Another blush. "She said I could sleep in her guest room. And to come over whenever I need to."

"Need to?" I repeated.

He looked at me, those blue eyes pleading. "Emma, you got to admit this is dangerous—you *got* to let me take care of you!"

I sighed. If I couldn't avoid him, I might as well let him make himself useful. Maybe he could find out something about what the police were doing. "Have you talked to the Sacramento police?" I asked.

"Yeah." He looked at me reproachfully. "You haven't gone

in and been interviewed by a detective. They got no one assigned to you."

"No. There was no available Saturday when I went in to be photographed—someone is supposed to call me."

He scowled.

"I'll probably get a call today," I reassured him. "If not, I'll call them."

He seemed content with that and attacked his toast with renewed vigor. "You got any jelly?" he asked.

I didn't. "Is honey okay?"

"Sure. Maybe some peanut butter, too."

I obliged, and watched as Vince fashioned the remaining pieces of toast into peanut butter and honey sandwiches.

Vince is a big man, and probably accustomed to having a much more substantial breakfast. I apologized.

"No problem," he said cheerfully. "Next time I come, I'll stop first and pick up a dozen eggs."

My heart sank. The expression on my face must have made my feelings clear.

"Aw, Emma." Vince pulled his notebook out of his pocket, waving it as if to indicate its value to me—and, by implication, him. "I got information from the report on Esther Vajic," he offered.

"I've been wanting to know," I admitted. "How did he kill her?"

"According to the police report, she died from a blow to the side of the head."

"Go on," I said.

"Apparently the Vajic woman had just arrived home, sometime between eight and nine o'clock. Her place was at . . ." He consulted his notebook. "13th and V Streets."

I knew where Esther lived. The area is mostly filled with apartments built just before or after World War II. But she had an older place, part of a cluster of little one-bedroom houses, all separate and arranged around courtyards. Sweetheart cottages, they used to be called. They were almost always well constructed, with hardwood floors and little fireplaces. Most of them had their own little gardens. A lot of these were built in the early thirties, with the notion that the typical tenants would be newlyweds; in reality, most were occupied by older women living alone. Nowadays they're mainly occupied by Asians, who grow astounding quantities of vegetables in the small garden plots.

"You know the neighborhood?"

I nodded.

"Okay. Her apartment is served by a separate row of garages, along the alley—open garages, stalls with roofs and sides. You can't close them up and lock them."

I imagined Esther, unprotected, making her way from the garage area to her little apartment.

"She'd apparently gone around to the back porch entrance to her place," Vince went on. "At least that's where she was found."

"The next morning?"

"Yeah." He laboriously turned the notebook pages with his peanut-butter-and-honey sticky fingers. "One of the neighbors saw her, an old Chinese lady who was out there real early to water her yard. The victim was on the walk, right next to the porch steps." He looked up at me. "She fought him—had on a jumpsuit and it was pulled off at the shoulders."

I remembered what the man had done to me—surprise first, then pain. He'd probably come up behind her, grabbed her, pulled down the jumpsuit to immobilize her arms.

"How did he kill her?"

"You know those wands they use to turn on lawn sprinklers? The old-fashioned kind?"

I nodded. I knew—a metal rod about a yard long, with a handle at the top and the other end rigged with metal fingers to turn a sprinkler control set in a little box on the ground. Frannie used to keep one by the front porch and one for the back. But she has a new sprinkler system now, on a timer.

"There was one of these wands by the side of Esther's porch rail. The way the police think it happened, she resisted and he grabbed the nearest available weapon."

"How . . . how did he hit her?"

"Caught her right across the temple."

I tried to visualize the struggle. A sprinkler wand isn't a short range weapon. There must have been some push and shove, then he'd stood back and flailed away, the same as I'd done with the flashlight.

Vince folded his notebook with the air of one who wants to close a subject. "Must have scared him that he killed her," he added. "The woman wasn't raped."

The Stalker . . . scared? It seemed incomprehensible. And right away he attacked a second victim? I shook my head. "Maybe I just don't understand rapists."

"Huh?"

"How come they're so sure it was the Stalker?"

"Identifying characteristics," Vince said curtly. "Smell of gasoline on her clothes. Faint but positive—those are the exact words in the report." He stuffed the notebook into his shirt pocket.

Until Saturday night's newscast, I'd been so certain Esther had been killed by whoever sent the letter. But maybe I was experiencing denial—maybe it was too unsettling to think I'd been attacked by a man who'd just killed someone else.

Vince drank a last cup of coffee while I filled him in on what had happened over the weekend, starting with the twin incidents of the dead rat and Anne's fright in the alley and concluding with yesterday's vandalism. "At least, toad man is identified now. He's a jerk named Benny Podesta."

As soon as I mentioned the name, Vince had his notebook out again.

"P-O-D-E-S-T-A," I said. "We haven't any proof, but he's got to be the same guy who—golly, why didn't I think of it?"

"Think of what?"

"The pink ribbon. That's Podesta's motive."

Vince looked at me uncomprehendingly, the stubby pencil poised over his notebook.

I explained about last year's demonstration, with pink ribbons on the portapotties, and how it was Podesta who'd caused the demonstration to turn nasty. He'd shown up with a dump truck and made as if to run down the Jobs First protestors. "He wanted us to know it was him, all right—he must be really focused on Jobs First. Why else would he go to the trouble of finding a pink ribbon to tie the rat to the doorknob?"

Vince took this as yet another indication of how much I needed his protection. "The guy's not that Sacramento Stalker, but he's a nut case. With someone like him on the loose, you *need* me. I got to work a shift tonight, and the day shift tomorrow, but then I'm coming back."

Thanks a heap, Frannie. But I managed a smile for Vince. Then, I thought, why not ask him to check on the Muellers?

Frannie had fobbed off another of Mueller's brochures on me last night at the coffee shop. I showed it to Vince, explaining my worries about Frannie falling for their malarky. We both noticed at the same time that the brochure was set up for use as a mailer, with a Washington, D.C., postal box number as a return address, and, beneath, a local address stamped in purple ink—a post office box in Ione.

"I didn't notice whether the stuff Frannie showed me Saturday had a return address," I said. "I'm pretty sure I would have noticed the purple ink. They must have put this on for the ones handed out at the seminar."

"Okay," Vince said. "I'll check into it. Mind if I take this?"

"Fine."

He folded the brochure and stuffed it into his pocket along with the notebook.

After he left I went back to thinking about the purple-stamped address on the brochure. It was odd that they'd have an address in Ione. The town, originally known as Bedbug, started out as a Gold Rush camp and was about thirty miles up in the foothills. Why would the Muellers headquarter themselves there? Maybe because the town's name went with the Corinthian Foundation's neo-classic image. More likely, I thought, because Ione was out-of-the-way—and definitely low-rent.

Ione—nee Bedbug—might well be worth a visit.

$\triangledown$

2 0

CORINTHIAN FOUNDATION: THE NAME conjured up images of stately classic buildings with porticos and columns across their fronts. The reality, I expected, would be different. The Jobs First office could do without my patrol services for one more day. In any event, I hadn't promised to start before tomorrow, when my clean-out job started.

My first stop in Ione was at the post office. I hoped the clerk might be obliged to give out information about postal box holders, or could be swindled out of it with a little freewheeling conversation. As soon as I parked I peeled the A-1 Salvage magnetic sign off the door of my truck—no sense playing detective with a sign on my door that had my name and phone number on it.

I was still standing beside the truck, the sign in my hand, when Mueller's Chrysler pulled to the curb across the street. *Bingo!* I tossed the sign into the back and climbed into the cab of the truck to wait and watch.

It was not Mueller who got out of the Chrysler. I supposed it was the chauffeur. He was a muscular fellow, pot-bellied and balding, with a fringe of gray-brown hair curling around the edges of his pate. He had the look about him of a former boxer, or, I thought more likely, a bouncer. He wore a white T-shirt with a pack of cigarettes in one turned-up sleeve and cheap polyester slacks that bagged at the knees—*definitely* not Mueller.

The man went around to the car trunk, opened it, and began taking out boxes. Brochures, I imagined, Corinthian Foundation propaganda for the outgoing mail. He stacked four boxes on the curb, then closed the trunk, picked them up and went inside.

I waited.

He took his own sweet time, but eventually came out, got into the car, and pulled away from the curb. I turned around in the wide street and followed cautiously—an old battered truck like mine is pretty good cover in this neck of the woods, but it's not invisible.

The Chrysler turned off on a side road. I didn't dare follow immediately, but went on past and then came back. I left plenty of distance, and worried each time the big gray car disappeared around a corner or over a hill. At last, I rounded a curve just as the car turned into a driveway.

I had to smile. Forget porticos and dignified columns— Chez Mueller was a doublewide mobile home. Nearby was an old barn, the Chrysler just now coming to a stop in front of it. There had been a farmhouse here once, on the site now occupied by the mobile home—the remnants of a hedge and an occasional fence picket or two indicated the outlines of the old garden. The mobile home looked as if it had been recently installed here, as did a metal-roofed carport that stood nearby, housing Madame Chignon's Taurus.

The chauffeur got out and dragged open a large pair of doors at the front of the barn, then propped them in place with two-by-fours. He drove the Chrysler in.

The place was isolated, surrounded by disused-looking grazing land. There were few trees—no place to park unseen and observe the Corinthian Foundation goings-on. For a moment I was frustrated, then I spotted a stretch of barbed wire fence in bad repair just opposite Mueller's driveway. What luck!—I would be Mueller's "neighbor," here to mend the fence.

I put on my old straw hat, and then began taking gear out

of my toolbox: wire cutters, pliers, extra coils of wire. I took out a hefty crowbar, too. A lady can't be too safe, as Vince has so often pointed out.

I studied the mobile home and the barn. The latter had recently been remodeled; a stairway went up along the outside, apparently to a second story room. I'd scarcely started fiddling with the fence when Mueller emerged from the upstairs part of the barn and stood on the landing.

"Hooper!"

No answer. I couldn't see the chauffeur, he was inside the barn.

Mueller yelled again. "Chrissake! Where are you?"

Hooper poked his head around the corner of the open barn door as Mueller, still shouting, started down the stairs. "The mailing labels for the quarterly, man. Christ! Where are they?"

So much for Frannie's *charming gentleman*. I edged farther along the fence to get a clearer view. Hooper, his movements suggesting a weary patience, handed Mueller a box. Mueller went back up the stairs.

I'd fiddled with the barbed wire for only few more minutes when Mueller started hollering again.

"Hooper!"

The driver again appeared at the barn's double doors.

"The printer's buggered. Where's Rachel? Tell that bitch to get her ass up here again and this time fix it right."

Wait 'til Frannie heard about this! She placed so much store on Mueller's courtly manners, the way he'd gallantly helped his wife from the car at the conference center last night. The man was not only a con artist, but a foul-mouthed bully.

▽

21

I<small>T WOULD BE A</small> pleasure to tell Frannie about what I'd seen in Ione—once I found a way to get her to listen. I headed straight for home and was there shortly after noon.

Frannie's Mercedes wasn't in the garage. She was most likely off on another of her shipping sprees, I thought. Upstairs, the blinking light on my answering machine indicated I'd had two calls. I pushed the PLAY MESSAGES button.

Kitty Hackett had phoned to inform me there would be a Jobs First meeting that afternoon. "We've got to make plans for the exhibit this weekend—and our Biblical correspondent has sent another letter. It's full of the same kind of stuff." A pause, as if she were considering the letter's content. "Well, you'll get the full gist of it this afternoon."

I resolved to be at the meeting.

The second message was from the Sacramento Police Department, a Lieutenant Douglas Laughlin of the Sexual and Child Abuse unit. He asked me to come in for an interview. "This afternoon, if at all possible," he added.

I called Kitty and told her I had to go to the police department before I came to the meeting, but would be there as soon as I could. Then I asked about Benny Podesta.

"The police haven't caught up with him yet. He may be stupid, but he's sly as a fox—no insult intended to the wild

101

canines." She chuckled, humorlessly. "Maybe he'll show up during our meeting. We could conk him over the head and hold him until the police get there."

I reminded her that I would begin my surveillance of the office tomorrow. "For what it's worth," I added. "I'm sure I'd recognize our friend Benny if I saw him skulking around—I just wish spotting our Bible-quoting correspondent would be as easy. That one scares me even more than Podesta."

"Me, too."

I fixed myself a late lunch and went down to get my truck out of the garage. Frannie was still gone—a major shopping spree, I thought. It's one of the ways she works off tension.

I had to wait at the police station nearly half an hour before Laughlin could see me. He was perhaps sixty, saggy-paunched, with colorless thin hair. We went through the same details I'd given the young blonde giant. When the interview seemed nearly over I mentioned my clothes.

"When can I have them back?"

He closed the file folder. "We return all property. In due time."

I asked whether my case was considered part of the Sacramento Stalker investigation.

He turned uneasily away and gazed out the office window and began methodically scratching his scalp. "I'm not at liberty to tell you that—not while the investigation is under way." He continued gazing out the window. He continued scratching, too—with both hands starting at ear level on each side and working around toward the back of his head.

I tried another tack. "I've wondered whether that man attacked me because I was with the Women Take Back the Night march."

"Um." Having finished the bottom row of head-scratching, Laughlin started over, this time about two inches above his ears.

I was determined to wring something useful from this interview. "I have another idea about why I might have been attacked. I've been helping out with this women's group—I went along on the Women Take Back the Night march because of them. You've heard of Jobs First?"

He nodded, still gazing out the window. "Um."

"I suppose you know the Jobs First office was vandalized yesterday—by Benny Podesta. Before that, Podesta was threatening us in bizarre ways. For instance, he left a freshly eviscerated rat on the office front door. Maybe you knew about that."

He turned back to look at me with an expression of mild interest.

"We're also getting threats of an entirely different sort."

"Um?"

"Someone—I'm sure it's not Podesta—is sending us letters. They're full of Biblical quotes, addressed 'to the harlots.' They're warnings. We should stay home, what we do is evil. We just got a second letter."

"Have these letters been reported to our department?"

"Yes. At least, I know the first one has. Kitty Hackett turned over the original—we kept a copy."

"Um." More scratching.

"It seems to me that there might be a connection here, between the threats we've been getting and the Sacramento Stalker." The minute I'd said it, I knew how far-fetched it sounded. Someone as dirty and smelly as the man who attacked me couldn't possibly have written those letters.

Laughlin turned his chair back, facing his desk. He fiddled with the clutter on it. "I'm sorry," he said tonelessly, "we don't comment on cases under investigation." He stood up and offered me a routine handshake. "We'll be in touch, Mrs. . . .um . . ."

"Chizzit."

"Be sure," he added, "that someone in your organization reports any further threats."

I gave him the response he deserved. "Um," I said.

$\triangledown$

22

I ARRIVED AT THE Jobs First office only a few minutes late. The words "STUPID BITCHES" were still scrawled on the outside of the building, but now they looked scrubbed-over and somewhat faded. A paint job was needed here— I'd have to see if I could get to it.

The front office was neat, with no sign of the damage Podesta had inflicted except for empty places where the potted ferns had been. I hollered a *hello* and shouldered aside the curtain to the back room.

Brenda and Kitty were seated at the work table with Coretta Vajic and Lois Muldoon. Brenda, in blue jeans but with her Katharine Hepburn topknot nicely done up, motioned me in.

"Glad you're here," she said. "Be patient, we're still making plans for next weekend."

They were deep in a discussion about *outreach* for the Women Working Wonders exhibit. I listened while rapid-fire decisions were made about telephone trees, publicity ploys, and ways to solicit more display items. As I listened, I gathered the exhibit was to be held at Lois's newly opened art gallery in Old Sacramento—I'd been wondering what they'd do about getting a place on such short notice.

Anne wasn't here. She must be at work, I decided. Lois

had said she worked a late shift—data entry for the Department of Motor Vehicles, or something similar. Lois had been trying to encourage her to try for something with more future in it, but, I gathered, was running into stiff opposition from Tony. It figured.

Kitty, who was wearing a tailored suit and blouse, was apparently taking a time-out from her day's duties. Lois, as always, wore a soft-looking tunic and pants and an abundance of wooden beads.

Coretta looked terrible. Her lipstick was almost gone, her lips rimmed in a deep brownish-red. Rouge and eyebrow pencil stood out against her pale skin; tortoise shell combs anchored her long hair, pulled severely back. She wore a stark white shirt and black slacks. I wondered why she was here. Maybe, I decided, it was easier than staying home alone.

I turned my thoughts to the business of the letters. Kitty hadn't said if there were specific threats—something to indicate the writer's intent. I wondered if this letter were addressed the same way the first one had been. "To the harlots"—our letter-writer had a decidedly warped view of what Jobs First was all about.

Kitty had joked about that earlier. "At least it's different," she'd said. "Usually they say we're lesbians."

Lois interrupted my thoughts.

"So . . . will you do that for us, Emma?"

"I'm sorry—what?"

"On Friday. Help unload the borrowed exhibit stands? At my gallery?" She gazed at me expectantly, a pencil poised over her clipboard. "The stands should be there by midmorning. We have to have them assembled by the time the exhibit items start arriving that afternoon."

"Sure thing." My clean-out job, which started tomorrow, should be long finished by then—even with taking time out to watch over the office.

Brenda cleared her throat. "Let's go back to the safety rules," she said. She turned to me. "We were talking earlier about Benny Podesta, and the threats in those letters," she said. "To begin with, no one works here alone." She glanced at Kitty, Lois, and Coretta in turn, then back to me. "Absolutely no one."

"That goes for working at the gallery as well," Kitty added.

"We'll try to be on the look-out, too," Brenda said. "Now, my husband will check the neighborhood a few times each day, between classes. And Tony Krouse has promised to keep an eye on us."

Those two? As far as I was concerned that translated into *not much help*, because Al Friedman would probably be busy with his classes, and *no help at all*, because Tony was who he was.

"Emma, how far away is that job of yours?"

"Just up the street. Remember the place that used to be the Magic Sewing Machine Center? I've been hired to clean it out."

My surveillance wouldn't be of much use, either. Brenda and Kitty were smart enough to know that; maybe they just wanted the others to feel reassured. "I can walk down this way from time to time," I said, "come by on the street and then return by the alley, or vice versa. And I can drive my truck down at noon, park in the alley to eat my lunch, that sort of thing."

"Good," Brenda said, sounding altogether cheerful—but she was nervously crumpling and uncrumpling an empty Benson and Hedges package.

"What did the police say they would do about those letters?" I asked.

Brenda shrugged. "For all practical purposes, nothing. What can they do?"

She was right, I thought. Even a twenty-four-hour watch on each of us—by professionals—wouldn't guarantee our safety.

Brenda looked at the crumpled cigarette pack, then tossed it expertly into the garbage bin.

No one said anything for a few moments.

Kitty broke the silence. "I've got copies of those letters for all of us," she said, tapping a manilla envelope on the table in front of her.

I was eager to see the letters, the first one, too—I hadn't

yet had the chance to look at it.

Kitty handed around the copies. They'd been marked *Letter # 1, Rec'd Friday* and *Letter #2, Rec'd Monday.*

The letters had identical inscriptions at the top, the lines of smallish type centered, letterhead style.

> *To him who overcomes, I will give the right to eat from the tree of life, which is in the paradise of God. (Rev. 2:7)*
>
> *To him who overcomes and does my will to the end, I will give authority over the nations. (Rev. 2:26)*
>
> *To him who overcomes, I will give the right to sit with me on my throne. (Rev. 3:21)*

Complete authorization from on high—that's what Kitty had said when she'd read the first letter to us. She was right. It was like a pre-printed letterhead, the letter-writer was submitting *proof* of authorization. From God.

I read the first letter through.

"It seems to me these letters have to have been written by someone with a tidy mind—the Biblical chapters and verses are all so carefully noted, and in ascending numerical order," Lois said. "Almost a scholar's mind," she added, and immediately looked as if she wished she hadn't said it.

I was more interested in the main body of the letters.

"To the harlots," the second one began.

> *I am the Spirit, and yet you do not know it! By my actions I am become the spirit who will eat of the tree of life and sit with my Father on his throne. You wallow in the filth of your desecrations of the sacred vessel that is Woman. Your acts are abominations. You do not yet fully know the terrible wrath of Righteousness, nor the extent to which you will weep and wail. It is too late for Repentance.*

"Hmmmm . . . eat of the tree of life," Lois mused when I'd finished reading it aloud.

"Oh, this is terrible," Coretta exclaimed loudly. "Abominations . . . filth." She put her hand to her mouth, and gazed out the window.

"Let's go on to the signature lines," Kitty said quickly. "Did you notice they were both the same?"

They were.

I AM THE SPIRIT WHO SHALL OVERCOME YOUR WICKEDNESS.

"Look at the quotes down at the bottom of the second letter," Brenda said quietly.

She held a golden cup in her hand, filled with abom-
inable things and the filth of her adulteries. (Rev. 17:4)
They that were brought up in scarlet embrace dung-
hills. (Lamentations 4:5)

I couldn't help but remember what Esther was wearing the night she was killed. A red jumpsuit.

$\triangledown$

23

F RANNIE'S MERCEDES WAS STILL absent from the garage that evening at suppertime. She pulled in a little after nine—the timing confirming my notion she'd been on a shopping spree. I'd have to admire every purchase she'd made before I could find an opening to bring up the subject of the Muellers; even so, I expected I'd have an uphill job.

I hurried down my stairs, encountering Frannie as she unloaded bags and boxes from the car trunk.

"Oh, I'm so glad to see you, Emma. Here, would you carry these for me?"

I followed her into the bedroom with a double armload, all the while considering a suitable opening. I dumped my bundles on her bed. "I went for a ride today."

"Oh? That's nice. You need to get out and have a nice time more often." She pulled a dress out of one of the bags and stood in front of the mirror, holding it in front of her.

I knew she was waiting for me to comment about it. I didn't.

"Do you like this?" she said finally. "I've been needing a transitional cotton, you know, and I thought dark blue might be a good change for me. It's sort of businesslike, don't you think?" She turned from side to side, checking her image. "I'm going to wear it for the seminar Thursday night at the Tolversons'."

I wondered how she'd finagled it. "That's something I
want to talk to you about, Frannie. I mean, I want to talk to
you about the Muellers."

She let me catch her eye briefly in the mirror, then again
avoided my gaze, feigning preoccupation with her new dress.

"I took a trip to Ione this morning."

"Ione? It's so pretty up there this time of year."

"Ione," I insisted grimly. "You know. Where the Corinthian Foundation is, and—"

"Look!" Frannie said, putting a lot of brightness into her
voice. "I bought a briefcase." She held the dress to herself
with one arm, picking up the slender briefcase with the other
hand. "I didn't want to get anything too big, you know, just
a nice little one. I *do* want to look businesslike."

I eyed the briefcase, saying nothing.

"Looking businesslike is so important, don't you think?"

I kept my silence, feeing my aggravation mount.

Frannie turned from the mirror. "So," she asked brightly,
"did you find the Corinthian Foundation? What does it look
like?"

"I didn't like the looks of it at all. I didn't find any
Foundation. All I saw was a mobile home and an old barn."

Frannie looked at me, startled.

"A ratty setup if I ever saw one," I added.

Frannie looked quite blank for a moment; then she ad-
vanced toward me. "Oh!" she said angrily. "Oh!"

"You really don't know a darn thing about your precious
Muellers," I told her.

"Oh! Shame on you!" She shook her finger right in my
face. "You, Emma, of all people! How dare you put the
Muellers down over what kind of home they have!" Her eyes
were large, glittering with tears.

I'd blown it. I waited before I spoke, hoping against hope
to salvage the conversation. "Maybe," I said softly, "I started
with the wrong part of it."

"You certainly did! Good Heavens, Emma! You—"

"Okay—okay! Frannie, I apologize. But the point is, I

don't think this outfit is all it's cracked up to be. I don't think you know—"

"I know enough!" Frannie whirled away from me, to stare into the mirror. "I know enough about this . . . *outfit!*" She drew a deep breath. "Emma, you should know better. You've met the Muellers. You've talked to them. You've seen how magnificently Carl treats Rachel. You know they are sincere, gracious, lovely people."

"But—"

"Don't *but* me any *buts*, Mrs. Suspicious. The Muellers are working very hard for what they believe is right. And, I might add, that's the same thing you've said about Brenda Friedman and her Jobs First organization . . . *outfit.*"

"Frannie—"

"I'm not through yet! I want you to know that just because the Muellers don't have a nice home—for Heaven's sake, they probably *chose* not to spend money on a home, so they can use it in other ways." She paused. "Even you should be able to understand that."

I said nothing, determined not to make things worse.

"And, just for your information . . .' " Frannie, still looking into the mirror, jabbed fiercely at a wayward curl, tucking it into place. "I've enrolled in Rachel's contribution program for family projects. I'm in the silver circle of donors. You have no idea of the prestigious names she showed me— important people who are in our same silver circle." She turned, staring fiercely at me. "Now! Not one more word—I won't listen to another word against Rachel and Carl."

I turned on my heel and left. As far as I was concerned, Frannie could play ring-around-the-silver-circle to her heart's content.

Later, when I got to thinking things over, I knew I shouldn't have been surprised at Frannie's reaction. But I was surprised—and disappointed—that the Tolversons were going along with all this.

24

T HE NEXT MORNING, TUESDAY, dawned bright, clear and sunny. I was up early, eager to be started on my clean-out job.

I made a quick inspection of the Jobs First office. After circling through the alley at the back, I came around to the front and pulled to the curb on the opposite side of J Street. Everything at the office looked serene and proper, except for the washed-out letters still scrawled on the building front.

At this hour almost all the parking spaces were empty. Only a few cars whizzed past on the street, which is one-way leading out from downtown and heavily used only during the afternoon commute. Nearly all the businesses along this section of the street were still closed, some with iron grill-work pulled across the fronts.

There was no sign of humanity up or down the sidewalk in either direction on the office side of the street. On my side, on the corner, was a combination bakery and take-out shop. As I sat watching, a woman emerged with a steaming container of coffee. She crossed the street, wearing a closed, guarded expression, and vanished into a nearby office. A bearded and groggy-looking man, his tattered sleeping bag loosely rolled under one arm, crawled from behind a clump of bushes at the front of the same office—his presence, I supposed, explained the woman's wariness. The man ambled past the truck, eyeing me briefly. I stared back; he averted his gaze.

Having had enough of J Street's early-morning ambience, I put the truck in gear and pulled away from the curb, heading toward the former Magic Sewing Machine emporium. I parked in the alley behind it.

I was curious to see what was inside. The money I get for cleaning and hauling off trash is adequate for my time and trouble, but it's the unexpected find—something of value on the antique or "collectibles" market—that makes the real money for me. I hoped there might be some good stuff still here. I might find a treasure trove in the recesses of the loft or in some long-forgotten cubbyhole. And I remembered having been in the store's basement, years ago. Old treadle machine heads, from decades of trade-ins, I supposed, had been stacked like cordwood across the length of the basement wall. If they were still there, I had a bonanza.

Before I went inside, I looked uneasily up and down the alley. The neighborhood here was much the same as at the Jobs First office, except the buildings were older; it was closer to downtown. I dug in my tool box for my new flashlight—metal, every bit as solid as the old one—and let myself in through the back door.

I found the circuit breakers, and turned on the electricity and then the lights. I stood looking around for only a few moments before I headed down the basement staircase.

At the bottom I stood under the weak flare of light from a single globe hanging from the ceiling. I'd bought into another disappointment; the sewing machine heads were gone. I stepped forward, swinging the flashlight beam here and there. The room was barren, picked clean—not even an old bobbin left.

I shone my light along the double row of two-by-fours that had once underlain the wall of stacked sewing machines. The row of boards started by the staircase and ran the entire length of the basement toward the front of the building, disappearing in dimness. I moved forward, shining my light to inspect the boards and the space behind them. They were still marked with indentations from the weight of all those vanished sewing machines.

Near the front of the building were the recesses of an under-the-sidewalk storage area, lit from above by dim outdoor light showing through glass roundels. Underground rooms like this are common in the older part of downtown. When the city was new—a jiffy-built point of debarkation for the gold mines—buildings were put up without much thought of floods. But the town's early citizens soon learned that the Sacramento River went on a rampage every few years. They solved the problem by raising the buildings on jacks or converting the first floors into basements. They filled in the streets to the new "ground level," but not the spaces under the sidewalks. According to Sacramento legend the under-the-sidewalk rooms sometimes served as secret passageways, used by thieves, prostitutes, opium addicts, and rumrunners. I suppose some passageways existed, especially when two or more of the narrow lots were held by the same owner, but I expect the space beneath the sidewalks was usually blocked off at the lot lines. Any old-time merchant canny enough to take advantage of the extra storage space was also wise enough to keep his merchandise secure.

I stepped forward and angled the flashlight beam this way and that, peering into the farthest recesses of the under-the-sidewalk room. As nearly as I could see, the space was sealed at both ends.

I went back upstairs.

The remainder of the building offered nothing but junk and debris: the decrepit hulk of a wooden display case I'd have to knock apart before I could haul it away, scattered stacks of old business forms, smelly rags, a crumbling styrofoam chest. At least, I thought, I'd have the consolation of being able to have the whole place done in one day—and I'd bid the job on the basis of two days' work.

I went back out to my truck for a crowbar and my sledge. I'd decided to tackle the display case first, work on it a bit, then give myself a breather and take a stroll down J Street for another inspection of the Jobs First office. I'd enjoy the walk, but my watching over the office was pretty much pro forma—the odds of catching Benny Podesta in the act of wreaking further havoc were slim indeed.

The morning was warm with a light breeze, only an occasional scatter of elm leaves blowing along the alley to suggest the arrival of fall. I found a couple of old bricks and used them to prop open the back door of the Magic Sewing Machine Center—the place sorely needed some fresh air.

Inside, I'd just passed the staircase when I heard a slight sound from below. I tensed; the hair on the back of my neck prickled. I held my mouth open, turning my head, straining to hear. Nothing.

I wished I hadn't settled for just shining the light into those dim recesses of the area under the sidewalk. Was the room really sealed?

Fear washed over me. I clenched the sledge in my left hand, the crowbar in my right.

After a moment's thought I set down the sledge hammer and picked up my flashlight. Holding it awkwardly in my left hand, I stood at the top of the stairs, remembering Frannie's warnings. *You go off by yourself to those houses and who-knows-where . . . alone in those strange places.*

I took a few silent steps down the stairs.

I thought of Vince's earnest blue eyes, his constant pleading that I shouldn't take risks, that I should let him take care of me. Maybe he was right. I glanced uneasily behind me, at the door to the alley. I'd unthinkingly left it open. Sunlight streamed through it; my eyes had adjusted to the gloom and I could see nothing outside but a blinding glare.

I couldn't stand here like this all morning, I told myself. I took another tentative step, then plunged down the stairs. The flashlight's beam veered crazily. Hearing a scrabbling sound at my feet, I whacked with the crowbar—one-handed, awkward. More scrabbling, I shone the flashlight's beam in time to see at rat scurrying toward the protection of a stack of packing boxes under the staircase.

Fool!

I marched the length of the basement and gave the

under-the-sidewalk room a thorough inspection. The ends were indeed sealed off. I came quickly back upstairs, closed and locked the alley door, and then stood stock-still in the semi-darkness.

I breathed the familiar old-building smells of dusty floors, ancient newspapers, long-ago mildew. Always before these smells had conjured up anticipation of a valuable find, a day contentedly spent in physical labor, the occasional discovery of some interesting oddment. Now I sensed only danger. Podesta was still on the loose, the Sacramento Stalker, too. And there was the retribution promised by the zealot who was writing those letters.

Never before had I been afraid on the job. I felt a cold, resentful anger.

$\triangledown$

25

Resentment and anger were still with me when I arrived home that afternoon, but I'd made up my mind to exorcise the feelings by turning them into positive action.

I phoned Brenda and told her I'd be over at the Jobs First office first thing in the morning to paint the building front and obliterate the lettering. Pleased with myself, I hurried back down to the garage to assemble my painting equipment.

Sourpuss, seeming to sense a lift in my spirits, followed. He raced ahead of me from the bottom of the stairs to the garage door, then dashed inside the minute I'd opened it. He kept an aloof watch as I collected rollers and pans, brushes to cut in the trim, and a bucket, and put them in the truck cab. But when I'd taken down my roller extenders from the garage wall and started toward the truck, he twined under-foot and then dashed out of reach when I tried to pet him.

"You old fool!" I said, pleased as punch to see him feeling his oats.

I went upstairs for cleanup rags and some liquid detergent. Sourpuss leaped past me, taking the stairs three-at-a-time. Inside, he found an old twist-tie on the floor near the sink, and immediately began batting at it with his paw.

"You're too old for that," I told him, trying to sound gruff. He looked up at me, yellow eyes staring for a long, quizzical moment. Then, with one deft sweep of his paw, he sent the twist-tie across the linoleum and under the refrigerator.

"Rascal!"

I headed downstairs with the detergent and rags.

When I came back, Sourpuss was on the sinkboard. I'd left the lid off the butter dish; he was happily lapping butter.

"Scat!"

He leaped down, paws scrabbling against the linoleum as he sought to gain traction. He bolted toward the screen door, but at the last possible moment executed a quick right turn and leaped onto my pile of old newspapers, the force of his arrival carrying him and the top layer of papers onto the floor.

"Sourpuss—just look at you! Where's your dignity, you clumsy old fool?"

With great decorum, he walked a few steps away, ignoring both me and the pile of newspapers. He sat down and began an elaborate toilette.

I stood, hands on hips, to watch his performance. He'd begun in genteel fashion—a few discreet licks, all the while avoiding eye contact with me—but shortly he lost himself in the enthusiasm of the moment. He had one hind leg straight up like a flagpole and was industriously licking his flank, his pink tongue working steadily to create a patch of damp hair.

After a time he paused to look up at me. "You must understand," his look seemed to declare, "that the cat you see before you has absolutely nothing to do with the ungainly creature of a few minutes ago." It was not he who had made the impulsive leap—he'd had no part in *that* fiasco.

"It was some other cat," I said. "Right, Sourpuss?"

He paused. Another long look. One paw was in mid-air in front of him. His tongue was out—momentarily forgotten, abandoned mid-lick.

"You old fool," I said again.

I let him have the rest of the butter.

$\triangledown$

26

Sourpuss's antics had put me in a good humor. I decided on a walk around the neighborhood—it had been weeks since I'd been out and about to have a look at what was blooming in this yard or that.

I let myself out the back gate and started down the alley toward Twenty-second Street. I'd scarcely hot-footed it past Velma Patterson's back yard when I heard a fast-paced thudding of footfalls—Al Freidman, jogging.

I called out a greeting. He slowed, squinting at me curiously from behind his wire-rimmed glasses.

"It's Emma Chizzit," I said, "your neighbor. You met me at the services for Esther Vajic."

He nodded, jogging in place, his tank top dark with sweat, plastered to his skinny chest.

I'd been meaning to make an opportunity to talk with him, ask him if he'd like to come along with our Saturday hiking group. Brenda had told me he liked to take excursions up in the foothills to search for geological specimens—our hiking crowd has a couple of rather good amateur naturalists, but we're always looking for folks who might know a little extra about the terrain.

"Brenda tells me you're a professor at Sacramento State College."

He looked at me blankly, then leaned forward to brace both hands against a nearby telephone pole. He began pushing back, one leg at a time, to stretch his calf muscles.

"She says you often go out—you know, collecting."

"What?"

I was surprised—he seemed so startled. "Collecting trips," I said, "for geological specimens. Brenda told me you were a geologist."

He looked away, gazing at nothing in particular, his face twitching. For a full minute he kept his silence, and occupied himself by stretching his thigh muscles—standing like a stork on first one leg and then the other while he pulled back each foot.

I plunged along, feeling like a fool but nonetheless continuing as I'd originally planned. "I belong to a hiking group. We meet on Saturdays and . . . um . . . go up in the foothills sometimes. Or along the river . . ."

He looked at me as if he'd suddenly remembered his manners. He nodded to indicate attentiveness and put on a wan little smile.

"I was thinking," I finished lamely, "that our trips would be more interesting with a geologist along. Would you like to join us one of these Saturdays?"

He began jogging in place again—obviously not interested, obviously eager to be off. "Nice of you to think of me, Mrs. . . ."

"Chizzit. Emma Chizzit. Look, I don't want to keep you."

"Thanks," he said, his knees pumping up and down, "but I'm more or less scheduled for a while."

I watched in puzzlement as he sprinted off, his footfalls raising puffs of pale gray dust that lingered in the still air.

▽

27

I RETURNED FROM MY walk to find Vince's car parked under the porte cochere, and Vince and Frannie on the side porch in what looked like deep conversation.

Vince saw me first and gave an eager wave.

"Hello, Emma," Frannie said as I approached. She was being altogether cheery.

We hadn't talked since last night's argument about the Muellers; I didn't want to let her get away with pretending everything was hunky-dory. "Hello," I said with what I hoped was a notable lack of enthusiasm.

My glum response didn't faze her. "I was just telling Vince," she said brightly, "I've planned the nicest hot-weather dinner for the three of us."

"Oh?"

"We'll have a Spanish-style menu, won't we Vince?" She took hold of his arm, and looked up at him, smiling. "I've got all the makings for a tossed salad. And we'll have some crusty bread, and I've whipped up a nice little frittata."

"What's a frittata?" I asked.

"It's like a omelet," Vince said. "It's got zucchini and tomatoes and onions and stuff in it. And you let it cool down before you eat it."

"That's right!" Frannie almost twinkled. "Vince and I

121

have it all planned." She looped her arm through his and leaned back, gazing up at him with her best conspirator's smile. "We'll have sangría with it." She turned to me. "But I've got some iced tea for you, Emma." Frannie always gives consideration to the fact that I don't drink.

Vince, oblivious to the tension between Frannie and me, beamed happily.

"Now," Frannie said, in tones of stern instruction as if she were speaking to small nieces and nephews, "Vince will come in the house with me." She gave his arm a squeeze. "And we'll just give Emma a little chance to freshen up." With that, she whisked Vince inside.

Freshen up—pink ruffles would have made her happy. She was going to have to settle for a pair of slacks and the one white shirt I had in my closet.

I washed my face, combed my hair and put on some lipstick—and promised myself to be civil throughout supper. When I entered Frannie's kitchen a few minutes later, she was busily preparing vegetables for the salad. Vince was slicing French bread.

"Gracious! That was certainly quick." Frannie's implied message was clear—I hadn't gone to enough trouble. I suppose there's no cure for Matchmaking Fever.

Frannie's cooking had, as always, produced delicious results. The conversation was less substantial, Frannie chitter-chattering relentlessly. It wasn't until she got up to clear the table and bring our dessert that I had a chance for a private word with Vince.

"I went up to Ione yesterday morning after you left," I whispered eagerly.

"Jeez! You already found that Corinthian place? I was gonna help you do that, I got the address that goes with the post office box."

I shushed him, motioning toward the kitchen. "I spotted Mueller's car, with his chauffeur, and followed him." I lowered my voice further. "Nothing there but an old barn and a newly-planted doublewide trailer. But don't bring it up with Frannie, she doesn't want to hear about it."

"How come?"

"Let's just say she doesn't want to be confused by the facts."

"What did you find out?"

"Well, for one, Mueller's not the elegant gentleman Frannie thinks he is. The man's a closet swearer—and a bully. They're running a scam for sure."

Vince leaned forward eagerly. "You found stuff to prove it?"

I hadn't thought about that. "No . . . not really—just general impressions. But I'm convinced that the Muellers aren't legit."

"We got to be able to prove it," Vince said.

He was right, of course.

"I checked with the post office in Washington," Vince went on. "They gave me an address to go with that box number—I got a call in now to check it out," he said, his voice rising with enthusiasm. "If the address is a dud, maybe they been moving that Corinthian Foundation just two jumps ahead of—"

I grabbed Vince's arm and pointed toward the kitchen. Everything seemed terribly quiet out there.

"They probably been moving around the country," Vince continued, whispering. "They just took out the Ione post office box a couple of weeks back."

That figured.

"Maybe you and me can find out more," Vince went on, "Maybe the Muellers—"

I shushed him again. Frannie was coming back from the kitchen.

"Here we are!" she announced brightly—too brightly. "Ice cream, *pistachio deluxe*. It's a new flavor." She made a big fuss about presenting us with the ice cream.

Even Vince seemed to be aware that we were in the midst of an awkward moment. "Hey!" he said. "I almost forgot to tell you what I got on Podesta." He reached for his shirt-pocket notebook.

"Podesta?" Frannie glanced inquiringly at Vince, then at me.

"Benny Podesta," I said. "The man who has been threatening the Jobs First people. The police identified him by description when he vandalized the office."

"He's got a record," Vince said, "going back before the time he kicked up a ruckus over at that state college campus. Been picked up in possession of amphetamines . . . carrying a concealed weapon . . ."

"Gracious!"

"Lists his occupation as construction worker—currently unemployed. And here's the interesting part. Way back when, he started his own contracting firm in partnership with his wife. Then they split. She had to sue to get her share of the business—and guess which organization helped her?"

So Benny Podesta and Jobs First went back a long way.

Vince went on. "It's going to be a tough haul to catch Podesta," he said. "He has survivalist connections. The reports say he has links to that bunch of nuts up in Idaho who—"

"Oh, but I'm sure they'll catch him," I put in quickly. Frannie was looking absolutely dismayed. I glared at Vince, wishing I were sitting close enough to kick him.

It was too late.

Frannie turned to me. "Emma, there you go again—so sure they'll catch this awful man. You never see the danger in anything!" She was into it now full tilt, off and running with her standard lecture on how I always took too many chances, and shouldn't do the work I do. Or get mixed up with *causes*.

"That march! Heavens! Emma, you could have been killed!"

"Let's not talk about it, Frannie," I said.

Our evening broke up soon after that, more or less by mutual consent.

I most sincerely wished Frannie were as willing to take advice as she was to dish it out—and that she'd keep her frittata to herself.

$\triangledown$

28

THE FOLLOWING MORNING I made it a point to be up and gone long before Frannie's curtains were open. I backed my truck silently past the porte cochere and Vince's car, and headed straight for the Jobs First office.

I drove past it first, circled through the alley behind, and then drove past the front again before I parked beside the dumpster in the alley and let myself into the workroom through the back door. I was ignoring the agreement that none of us should be in the office alone, but I'd be spending most of my time out front. And I'd brought along my new "insurance policy"—the oversize metal-bodied flashlight loaded with four D batteries. It had a thoroughly satisfying heft.

Brenda, as she'd promised, had left two cans of paint on the battered work table.

I stood, flashlight in hand, and felt the first edges of nervousness. The locks in this place were a joke—somebody could be lurking in the front office. Clutching the flashlight tightly, I stepped forward and slid back the curtain separating the workroom from the reception area.

Morning light streamed through the storefront window. The rectangular "Women's Job Action Center" sign—outlined in silhouette—was centered in the window as precisely as before. Now, no longer flanked by the ferns Benny Podesta

125

had redecorated out of existence, it seemed skimpy and out of proportion.

I returned to the back room, my fear overcome by anger, and went to unload painting equipment from my truck.

A tired-looking Honda Civic, faded to a pale blue, had just pulled up. It was Anne—all smiles, wearing a pink T-shirt and a pair of paint-stained jeans. She said Brenda had told her I'd be painting this morning; she'd decided to help.

For Anne's sake, I tried to conceal my lack of enthusiasm. She'd been wanting a heart-to-heart; there was no backing away from it now.

I let her help me carry in the paint gear, and we'd just gotten inside when the phone rang.

I answered it. "Jobs First."

I heard nothing for a moment, then a guttural chuckle.

"Bitch," a low, growling voice intoned.

I should have hung up, but I wasn't about to relinquish the opportunity to become personally acquainted. This was Benny Podesta—destroyer of ferns, slaughterer of rats, collector of flattened toads.

"Podesta," I whispered to Anne.

The guttural chuckle came again, louder. It expanded into a rasping cackle—the bastard was enjoying himself!

"Stupid old bitch . . ."

Old!—he knew it was me. I stared in disbelief at the phone.

"Why don't you stay home, bitch?" His voice was thick, coarse with excitement. He was enjoying himself, getting off on this. I felt used.

"You got your last warning." His laugh cackled in the receiver. "You hear me, old bitch?"

I was rigid with anger, ready to explode.

He laughed.

"Podesta, you asshole! Buzz off!"

Silence—I couldn't even hear him breathing. Anne was staring at me, her eyes huge. "Buzz off!" I shouted, hating Podesta for bringing me to the point where I'd use such language.

I waited until he hung up before I broke the connection, then took a long, deep breath and slowly loosened my grip on the phone.

"I shouldn't let crumbs like Podesta get the best of me," I said to Anne. Maybe it was a mistake, I thought, to let him know he'd been identified.

"Oh!" Anne's eyes sparkled. "*You* got the best of *him*!"

I felt defeated, I'd let him bring out the worst in me. But, in one sense, Anne was right. My *macha* performance had probably worked—Podesta, intimidated when he hadn't encountered the cringing female he'd expected, would more than likely pull a disappearing act. Still, I asked Anne to phone the police.

While she was making her report, I went ahead and set up the painting equipment.

Anne emerged to report that the police had said they would have patrol cars in the neighborhood to keep an eye on us. Also, they'd need a statement from one of us for the file. I must have looked glum at the prospect of having to take the time. "I'll do it," she said.

We set to work quickly. I started with the long handled roller, at the right hand edge of the building. Anne took the paintbrush and began cutting in around the storefront window and the lower perimeter of the front wall. I noticed she looked rather pretty that morning, her strawberry blonde hair and fair skin emphasized by the rosy pink of her T-shirt.

She chattered for a while about nothing in particular. Give it time, I thought—the subject of Tony was bound to come up.

My attention strayed. I studied the occasional passing pedestrian and began to develop a fine fantasy: Podesta, swarthy skin, beak nose, hairy chest and all might have the *chutzpah* to come wandering by. If so, a citizen's arrest would be great sport—especially if we found it necessary to dump a bucket of paint over his head. To restrain him, of course.

"Emma . . ."

The tone of Anne's voice had changed.

"Emma . . . I was really embarrassed the other day." She

laid her paintbrush carefully across the rim of the paint can. "I mean, about Tony. It always hurts when he . . . gets like that."

She shifted uneasily.

"You don't have to let anyone hurt you," I said, and made a point of staring just below the sleeve of her T-shirt, where the bruise marks clearly showed on her arm.

She looked away, her face flushed.

"You don't have to let anyone hurt you," I repeated. "Not physically—and not any other way, either."

She still wouldn't look at me.

I turned my attention back to my work. I'd started from the right; my long up-and-down sweeps had reached as far as the "S" at the end of "BITCHES."

Anne shrugged. "It's just that Tony . . ." Her voice trailed away.

There was a long silence.

"I had to learn the hard way that no one has the right to hurt me," I said. "It wasn't easy. Growing up, I was always well treated—I didn't have to learn how to defend myself."

I pushed the roller up and down, sweeping away the last four letters of "BITCHES." I glanced down at Anne, who stared back eagerly, her eyes filled with trust. "My first husband was a nice man," I continued. "But after he died . . . well, let's just say I got a real education from my second husband." I paid a lot of attention to loading a roller full of paint, then made two sweeping strokes, obliterating entirely the word "BITCHES." "I told you about Ike the other day," I said.

"Yes." The word was barely a whisper.

"When I married Ike," I went on, "I thought he would be someone strong, someone I could trust—a partner, just like Robert. But he wasn't."

Ike hadn't been a grown man at all, I thought, just a boy in a man's body. I was certain Tony was the same, emotionally a kid whose ego depended upon being accepted by other kids—and the whole problem compounded by his drinking.

"You and Ike aren't married anymore," Anne said. She

was staring at her paint brush, as if she were addressing the remark to it instead of me.

"That's right. I divorced him."

"For . . . hurting you?"

Hurting me. Ike had never left bruises. Still, I suppose it was as good a way as any to sum things up—the drinking, how he treated me and the kids. My marriage to Ike was a disaster for Danny and Joanne. The effects still linger—with Danny in particular.

"Yes, he hurt me," I told Anne. I made an effort to push back the painful memories. "Let's get back to work." I said in a changed tone of voice, looking up at the freshly painted wall. "We can't be certain until it dries," I said, "but I think we're going to have the job done with one coat."

Half an hour later we stood back to admire our work.

"Emma . . ."

I waited. Here came the rest of it.

"You know . . . with Tony . . . it's not just the buddy thing." A pause. "It's not that simple. That meeting he was in—you know, next door?" She took a deep breath and looked up, her gaze straight into mine. "That was an A.A. meeting. Alcoholics Anonymous."

There was no point in pussyfooting. "I knew."

"You did?"

"Sure. Ike was in A.A.—almost the whole time I was married to him."

"Oh," she said. "I always thought that people couldn't . . . you know, *tell*."

"Most people can't. And anyone who can figure it out has already been there and won't cast any blame. Don't worry about it."

"I keep wondering." Another one of those pauses. "Tony is trying hard. I know he is, but . . ." Her voice trailed off.

Trying. How many times had Ike talked about how hard he was trying? "A.A. didn't work so well for Ike," I said.

"What do you mean?"

"Well, he was particular about the A.A. group he'd join. He'd go to one, and come home saying they were a bunch of

snobs. Then he'd go to another, and there'd be something
wrong with them, too."

She stared at me, a haunted look on her face.

"Eventually," I went on, "Ike always seemed to find the
kind of group he wanted."

Anne continued to stare at me. "What kind of group was
that?"

I decided to let her have it, flat-out. "Ike wanted a group
with backsliders, guys who would take turns falling down."

"Oh . . . well, Tony's group isn't . . ."

She blushed, and then opened her mouth to speak again.
But she didn't.

I waited. She studied her paint brush as if the wisdom of
the Universe were concealed in it.

"Tony's group isn't . . ." I prompted.

She looked up, startled, then pasted a bright smile on her
face. "Well, that one group of Tony's . . . Oh—Tony doesn't
belong to just this one group. He belongs to another group,
too. We call it the big group. It's got both men and women
in it. When we go—"

When *we* go. I caught that right away, and Anne realized it.

If drinking wasn't Tony's problem exclusively then I knew
why she continued to put up with him. I decided to offer her
a way to dodge the rest of this conversation. "The big
meeting is an open meeting?" When it's an open meeting,
anyone can attend.

"Yes," Anne whispered.

I'd gone with Ike to open meetings. He favored the kind
in shabby halls, cigarette smoke hanging thick in the air.
Shabby halls, shabby people—morally shabby. Nevertheless,
I'd met a few good folks and once in a while Ike would even
agree to go out for a soda afterward with some of them. That
was the part I thought could really help, making friends with
the ones who *weren't* backsliding. But the times he was
willing to do it were few and far between.

"In the big meeting," Anne said after a while, "Tony sits
with the men from his group, but he wants me with him,
too." Anne had been speaking quite rapidly. She took a deep

breath before she continued. "I belong to A.A. too."

I was about to tell her that was nothing to be ashamed of.
She abruptly raised one hand in mock greeting. "Hi!" Her
voice was unnaturally loud. "My name's Anne, and I'm an
alcoholic."

"Take it easy." I put an arm across her shoulder.

"But here's the good news." Anne's voice was constricted
now, as if her throat were tight with the effort not to cry. "I
haven't had a drink in six months."

"Congratulations!"

Tears overflowed, sliding down her cheeks. "I couldn't—
didn't *dare*—take a drink," she said. "Not since I joined Jobs
First. What if Brenda or Kitty or somebody saw me? I care
about them too much to . . . to . . ."

"I'm glad you quit. It doesn't matter why."

How was I going to find a way to end this conversation?

"It's funny," Anne said, her voice elaborately casual.
"Lately, Tony's been *really* down on our Jobs First group."

"How so?"

"He says that what we do is all wrong, that we're misguided—*pink ribbon misguided*. And he says we're . . . dumb."

"Maybe he's just jealous," I told her. "A man like Tony . . ."

"I wish Tony didn't want me to get up and talk in the big
meeting. He says that I'm a sissy, that I won't ever really . . .
not unless I can talk about things I did while . . ."

I fished a clean paint rag out of my back pocket and
handed it to Anne. She blew her nose.

"Tony says if you're really going to get well, you *have* to
tell."

"Hogwash!"

Ike and his cronies used to come up with lurid tales about
stuff they'd done drunk. You're supposed to *qualify*—that
means admit you're a drinker and that drinking has caused
you trouble. But Ike and his mates bragged. I'd always
thought there was something sick about it.

"Look at me," she wailed. "I can't go to pieces like this in
front of everybody!"

Lord knows, I thought, what humiliation Tony wanted

Anne to put herself through. He wanted her brought down
again—wanted to make sure she'd stay under his control.

"I'm sure you'll do just fine at the big meeting," I told her.
"You don't have to talk about things you're ashamed of—
just tell them how well you've done lately."

"You think that would really be all right?"

"Sure. You don't have to do it the way Tony says."

"You really think so?"

"Of course! In fact, I wouldn't mind being there, just to
watch how well you do."

"Oh!" Her face lit up. "The meeting's tonight. *Would* you
come with me?"

$\triangledown$

29

A͏FTER ANNE LEFT, I gathered my paint equipment and started for the truck. A white Volkswagen convertible pulled into the parking spot she'd just vacated. The car's top was down, there was no mistaking who was driving—Jonathan Lee—King of Smarm.

Lee got out, canvas satchel slung over his shoulder, every stitch of his wardrobe impeccably casual. He came toward me, extending his hand and offering a smile worthy of a television news anchor. "Jonathan Lee. Remember? KXPR Radio."

"Emma Chizzit, A-1 Salvage," I deadpanned. I didn't offer to shake hands.

He flashed his most ingratiating smile. "We talked at the memorial service for Esther Vajic, didn't we."

He hadn't missed my sarcasm. He ran a hand through his lank brown hair and looked off into the distance for a moment. Let him be uncomfortable, I thought. I started toward the truck with my armload of paint gear.

When I opened my tool bin he propped himself against the cab with a proprietary air, produced a tape recorder from the satchel and began fiddling with it. He didn't look at me, didn't ask any questions, just fiddled with his machine.

Forward. Fast forward. Rewind. I had the impression it was a deliberate tactic, something he did to make people

133

anxious about whether he was going to interview them. It wasn't going to work—I didn't give a fig for being interviewed. But Brenda seemed to think he was a useful publicity contact; I probably ought to lighten up a little.

"I suppose you want to interview me."

Lee gestured to the recorder, indicating he'd turned it on. "This is Jonathan Lee and this is September 12," he intoned. "I am talking with Mrs. Emma Chizzit and we are on the premises of Jobs First." He turned to me. "Now, Emma, let's get your statement on the record."

I bristled at his over-familiar use of my first name.

"Are you a member of Jobs First?"

"What do you want, Lee?"

He kept a perfect calm, although he ran his hand through his hair again before he turned to me with another of those ingratiating smiles. "I want to know . . ." He paused, as if deliberating, then apparently made up his mind. "I want to know if you were scared when you got the phone call from Benny Podesta this morning."

I disassembled the paint roller handle and carefully put it in the tool bin before I turned and confronted him.

"How did you find out about that?" I asked the question as casually as I could—never mind that his knowing about Podesta's call made me inexplicably angry.

He smiled again. "Perhaps I found out from the police."

"Do they make it a policy to tell you everything?"

"No." The smile was still in place.

I glared at him, suddenly aware that he was trying to use my anger to get me to say something I otherwise might not.

"So?" I said.

He shrugged. "So, as long as I'm investigating the Sacramento Stalker, whatever the police are doing is part of what I investigate."

He could have found about the phone call if he'd managed to make a few friends down at the police station, I supposed. Or maybe from the police radio if there had been any reports from the patrol cars that were supposed to keep an eye on us this morning.

"So tell me," Lee said. "Are you frightened of Podesta?"

I studied Lee, trying to fathom his bland expression. There seemed to be a common thread to all his interview questions. *Were you afraid?*

"Are you frightened of Podesta?" Lee persisted.

Fear. He zeroed in on fear, fed on it. I felt repulsed, but immediately clamped down on my emotions. "Why should I be afraid of Podesta?" I said, keeping my voice mild. "He didn't show up this morning."

"Ah," Lee said. "He hasn't shown up *yet*."

I wanted to be rid of this creep. "Why are you so focused on Podesta?" I asked. "I thought you were chasing the Stalker."

The smile was back again. "I've explained that," he said. "I'm interested in all aspects of violence against women."

30

MY RUN-IN WITH JONATHAN Lee left me in a foul mood, and my spirits weren't much improved when I arrived home and saw Vince's car still parked in the porte cochere.

Hoping to avoid being noticed by either Frannie or Vince, I pulled into the garage and closed the door behind me with as much dispatch as possible, then headed up my stairs on the double.

I stopped, startled, at the top step. Taped to my porch rail was an envelope. The paper was heavy—a rich, creamy pink. My name was written with a flourish on the front.

Inside was a note on the same sort of expensive paper, the message written in the same flowing script. "My dear Mrs. Chizzit," it began. I skipped down to the signature—Rachel Mueller. I might have known.

The note said she'd "just stopped by" and wanted a "little get-together." She'd come back later.

The woman just didn't give up!

I contemplated the sheet of smooth, heavy paper for a moment. I folded the note in half, then carefully folded back each side, twice, in a manner I'd learned in the third grade.

It made a splendid glider, although a bit stubby. "I name this craft *Mueller's Fortune*," I muttered under my breath, and sailed it downward. I'd aimed for the garbage can by the corner of the garage, but it swerved and then stuck, nose first, in the center of Frannie's back lawn.

I trudged down the steps, retrieved the glider, and started for the garbage can.

"You ought to be ashamed of yourself!"

It was Velma Patterson, hanging over the sideyard fence, garden hose in hand, a disapproving scowl on her face.

"That Mrs. Mueller is a fine, religious lady," she said, poking in my direction with the hoze nozzle. "I talked with her—with Rachel—when she came." She shook her head and jabbed the hose nozzle at my pink glider. "What you did—you shouldn't be so disrespectful. If you ask me—"

"I didn't."

"If you ask me," Velma repeated, bristling, "you ought to at least let her talk to you. The way you've treated her!—a fine Christian woman, and—" She broke off suddenly, looking in triumph toward the street.

I was trapped. The champagne-colored Taurus was just pulling to a stop at the curb. Unwilling to give Velma material for an on-going sniping action, I greeted my guest with cool politeness and escorted her up the stairs.

"Have a seat," I said, once I'd ushered Madame Chignon inside.

She had a choice between my rocking chair and one of the chairs by my kitchen table. She hesitated, then pulled out a chair by the table and sat, holding her purse primly in her lap. "My," she said, "your apartment is so . . . quaint."

"It suits me." I remained standing, beginning to enjoy her discomfiture.

I hadn't opened the windows earlier; my apartment was stuffy with the midday heat. I studied with satisfaction the rigidity of Rachel's posture, the film of perspiration on her upper lip. She was dressed in another of her form-fitting outfits. A smooth waistline and uplifted breasts don't come naturally on a woman of her vintage, so she had to be wearing uncomfortably warm foundation garments—a panty girdle at least, my guess, and an industrial strength long-line bra.

"Mrs. Chizzit, I am so glad I managed to find you at

home." Rachel's pasted-on smile was unwavering. "I hope you've studied the brochure I gave you about our special women's crusade." She batted her eyelashes at me encouragingly.

"No."

"Oh . . . well . . ." She set her purse on the table and began rummaging in it. "I suppose you've been busy—we're all of us so busy nowadays. A shame. We don't have time to focus on the really important . . ." She pulled out a brochure like the one she'd given me before.

I made no move to take it; I didn't want to get near her and risk being held by those manicured hands.

She set the brochure on the table. "Well, I'd much rather just *tell* you what we're doing. We must protect the family against the many threats that face it today, Mrs. Chizzit. That's why we have our women's crusade for the American family."

"A crusade? I'm impressed."

She was completely unaware of my sarcasm. "Oh, absolutely! We wage a two-pronged counterattack against the prevailing evils that—"

"Evils—what evils?"

"Oh, there's so much! Rock music—it has satanic messages, you know. Pornography is everywhere, even on television. Everywhere there are loose morals . . . single mothers living in sin, not caring what their children see or know." She shook her head. "Broken families are a terrible disaster."

"There are worse things," I said quietly.

She went on. "Divorce . . . selfish mothers who don't stay home to care for their children."

It was hard to keep my silence. I'd *selfishly* worked long hours to put food on the table for my kids—first when I was a young widow, and then when Ike was "between jobs."

"Mothers just don't belong in the workforce," Rachel said smugly. "Women can't earn enough to support a family, anyhow. And they shouldn't try."

I was hot under the collar—tempted to mention my involvement with Jobs First. "Sometimes women have to work," I said.

She pounced on that. "And it's a *shame*, isn't it?" She shook her head sadly. "*Such* a shame! But that's where we come in—we can provide help through our Organization for Democracy and the Family."

"No kidding. What does this organization do?"

"Oh, a great deal! A *great* deal, Mrs. Chizzit. We not only fund programs to thwart the many attacks on the family, we go to the heart of the problem with direct help—help that keeps families together and mothers at home. Here! Just *look* at this brochure." She scooped it up from the table and unfolded it. "Look at the pictures of all these beautiful children—rescued children, we call them." She held the brochure forth insistently. "We can give you the opportunity to rescue your own very own child by becoming a member of our Brigade of Honorary Grandmothers."

"What would I do, as a member of this . . . *brigade*?"

"Do? Oh! You would accomplish a great deal. Your contribution—"

"In other words, what I would *do* is contribute money."

"Yes." She smiled winningly. "And then your picture and the picture of the child you've rescued will appear in the very next issue of our *Family Quarterly*."

I wondered how much she'd gotten out of Frannie. Madame Chignon and her patriotic crocodile of a husband pocketed every dime they took in, I was sure of it.

The time had come to ease her out.

I heard heavy footsteps on the stairs outside—Vince! I moved quickly, and opened the door just as he was getting ready to knock. "I've got company." I gestured toward Rachel.

Vince, eager as always, missed the cue. "Gee, Emma, I'm glad I caught you home. I been doing some checking. I found out—"

"Come on in, Vince," I said loudly, "meet my guest." I turned, gesturing again toward Rachel.

Vince, still oblivious, kept on. "You should have told me you was going over to paint at the Jobs First office. I would have come and helped you."

Rachel's eyes flew wide open, a look that was almost apoplectic. Her face slowly suffused with a dark red.

"Vince," I said icily, and gestured toward Rachel, "I have company."

"Huh? Oh, Jeez."

"Mrs. Mueller," I said, "this is my friend Vince Valenti. Vince, this is Rachel Mueller."

Vince gaped, then recovered his equilibrium. He wiped his hands on his shirt front, preparing to offer a handshake.

She ignored him for a moment, shooting me a malevolent glance, as if I had been at fault for not saying something about Jobs First right away. Then Madame Chignon turned to Vince. "Hello there."

She turned her body directly toward him, focused on him entirely, everything pointing in his direction—her toes, her tightly-clamped-together knees, the twin turrets of her breasts, that everlasting smile.

She hadn't offered to shake hands. Vince brought his hands down to his sides and inclined his body forward—an embarrassed gesture halfway between a nod of the head and a bow.

"Mrs. Mueller was just getting ready to leave," I said.

Rachel still aimed herself at Vince. "Oh, but not before we have a chance to get acquainted." Her face had paled, giving her a stricken look despite her animation. I stared at her, astounded. She seemed to be on auto-pilot since Vince dropped the news of my involvement in Jobs First—a mechanical geriatric Barbie Doll. I wondered why she'd been thrown for such a loop. Surely she didn't believe her own propaganda; she couldn't, she'd have to know it was all a sham.

Vince shifted uneasily from one foot to another.

"What do you do, Mr. Valenti?"

"Vince, why don't you have a seat?" I said hurriedly, indicating the rocker.

Vince, looking non-plussed, sat down. He squirmed awkwardly—but in silence.

Rachel turned in her chair—toes in the high-heeled

pumps *en pointe*, knees high, twin turrets in perfect align-
ment. "I'm sure you must have an interesting job, Mr.
Valenti."

"Vince will be retiring soon," I said. It was the first thing
I could think of to keep her from finding out he was a
policeman. I shot Vince a meaningful glance.

"Uh . . . yeah," he said.

"Mrs. Mueller was about to leave," I persisted. I picked
up her purse and handed it to her.

Madame Chignon got up stiffly and left without saying
another word. Vince and I stood on the porch, watching her
walk down the driveway and out to her car.

"She makes me uncomfortable," Vince said.

I shrugged. "Come on in. I'll fix us some coffee."

He seated himself at the kitchen table, and took out his
pocket notebook. "Weird lady!" He shook his head in mys-
tification, and then apparently dismissed the subject from
his mind. He began thumbing through the notebook pages.
"Like I said when I came in, I been checking on the
Muellers." He looked up at me, beaming proudly. "I did a
little finagling and got a reading on their bank accounts."

"Great! What did you find out?"

"They got a swarm of accounts with fancy titles. Strong
America Corporation, Organization for Democracy and the
Family, Christian Unity Fund, Corinthian Foundation
Trust, and so forth—all of which operate on signature of
either Carl F. Mueller or Rachel J. Mueller. Ditto for a
personal checking account."

"Is there much money in these accounts?"

"Well, there's a lot of action. A fair amount of money, too.
It comes in mostly to the fancy-name ones—except Corinthian Foundation Trust. What happens is interesting. It's
regularly switched from all the others to the Trust."

"And from there . . . ?"

Vince grinned at me. "This Trust pays a monthly allow-
ance to the Muellers—living expenses."

"And?" I persisted.

"This is where it gets tricky," Vince said. "The Trust pays

big amounts to another account, Corinthian Associates.
And . . ." He gave me a significant look. "This Corinthian
Associates account is in the name of Carl F. Mueller only."

"What happens to the money in that account?"

Vince heaved a great sigh. "That's what I still got to find
out. Seems like there's Corinthian Associates accounts all
over the landscape. Checks go out from the Corinthian
Associates account here to Corinthian Associates accounts
in . . . let's see." He checked the notebook. "Oklahoma City,
Los Angeles area, Phoenix, Bakersfield, and Arlington, Vir-
ginia—that account's labeled National Corinthian Associates." He scowled. "Judging by the action on the accounts,
they were in Bakersfield just before they came here."

"I still got to find out the rest of it," he said. "Next stop,
the Bakersfield Police."

$\triangledown$

3 1

At five o'clock that evening, Anne phoned to remind me about the A.A. meeting. I agreed to rendezvous with her at a doughnut shop outside the meeting hall.

The meeting was in a bad neighborhood, which—considering what I knew about Tony—was altogether expectable. I searched for the address Anne had given me and at last found the doughnut shop she'd mentioned, smack-dab in the middle of a stretch of vacant buildings, stores with iron bars over the windows and parking lots strewn with trash. There was a bar across the street, OPEN AT 6 A.M. according to a neon sign over the door.

I could see Anne inside the doughnut shop, next to the window. She jumped up as soon as she saw me, and gave me an awkward hug. I returned it with as much grace as I could muster, considering my low level of enthusiasm for the evening ahead.

"Where's Tony?" I asked.

"He went to pick up Phil and Clarence."

"Then it's just you and me," I said, trying to sound jovial. I held out my arm, as if I were a gentleman preparing to escort his lady.

Anne giggled, took my arm, and directed me toward a mall corridor at the rear of the doughnut shop.

The meeting room was large, dingy, filled with rows of cafeteria-style tables—and as depressing as any A.A. meeting hall I could remember. There were windows along one wall, water-stained beige drapes pulled partly across them. The place smelled of sweaty clothes and unwashed bodies; there was a heavy pall of cigarette smoke.

Anne looked uncomfortable. "It's better where our women's group meets," she said. "There's nowhere near so many people."

There were forty people here already, at least. They milled around, setting up folding chairs and exchanging greetings. Coffee was being served in the back of the room.

I spotted one of the men from Tony's group heading in our direction, and nudged Anne. She stiffened.

"Hiya, Annie," he said, giving her waist a proprietary squeeze.

"Hello, Steve."

We moved away from him quickly.

"Tony and his group always sit at the end of this row, up near the front," she told me. "As soon as he's here, he'll be looking for me. He said we were to sit with him."

"We don't have to," I said. "Let's sit in the same row, but not too close."

She gave me an odd little smile. "Okay."

We sat down.

The meeting was starting, the same familiar routine. People were taking turns, standing and reading the Twelve Steps from tired-looking printed cards that had been distributed to each table.

"There's Tony," Anne whispered nervously.

I watched Tony as he made his way toward us—stage-whispering *hiya* right and left, punching shoulders and thumping backs. He moved steadily between the rows of chairs until he was behind ours. He took hold of Anne from behind, one hand on each shoulder, and gave her a squeeze and a shake.

"There's my girl!"

She sat perfectly still.

"Hey! Come on," he whispered urgently, and gestured toward the table where his buddies sat.

She turned to face him, her face carefully composed. "I'm sitting here with a friend. I told you she was coming. Tony, this is Emma Chizzit. You remember—from the Jobs First office?"

He glanced at me and nodded coldly.

"Both of you, then," he said to Anne. "Come on."

"We'd rather stay here," I said.

Anne chimed in immediately. "We're fine here, Tony. Really."

He glowered at me, then summoned up a lop-sided grin and glanced around the room. He balled his right hand into a fist, and dropped a light punch on Anne's shoulder. "Catch you later," he said tightly.

The first speaker had already begun, a man with a lean and exceedingly wrinkled face. His hair, dyed black but showing white at the roots, was slicked straight back. He had on a plaid shirt in faded tones of red, the sleeves rolled to his elbows to reveal an astonishing array of tattoos.

He said he'd been sober for twenty years, but he talked about his drinking days—a long and well-rehearsed ramble about sleeping in flop houses and having to pawn his work boots, and a complicated story about a bottle-gang buddy insisting it was okay to drink Sterno if you first strained it through a slice of rye bread.

Theme and variations, I thought. The same song, sung round and round in endless circles. A.A. could be better than this. This was the loser crowd, or at least a lot of the folks here were losers.

I looked over at Anne, sitting still and frightened-looking.

The next speaker had gotten up, a woman. "Hi, my name's Barbara," she began bravely. Her glance darted around the room, then held steady on someone behind me. I wanted to turn and look, but didn't.

The woman began to speak in a faltering voice of how guilty she felt about going to bars after work instead of going home to her daughter. "I'd stay and stay," she whispered.

"So drunk . . . sliding off the stools." She looked away from whoever it was behind me, then held her gaze steady again. "That's what makes me feel so ashamed. My little girl . . . all alone. I . . ."

The woman was in agony. I turned to look behind me. A tall, thin man with a shock of iron gray hair and piercing eyes sat erect, his gaze locked on her. The message in his look was obvious. *Go on . . . say it!*

The room was breathlessly quiet.

"And all the while my little girl," the woman whispered, "my poor baby . . ." She stopped, and began to cry.

A woman hurried to the front of the room, put her arms around Barbara. "We know, honey. It's hard," she said. I heard a sharp intake of breath from the man behind me.

The woman was whispering to Barbara. Barbara was shaking her head.

"She's just not ready yet." The woman led Barbara off to one side of the room.

I squeezed Anne's hand. I was about to tell her she didn't have to put herself through the same thing, but at that instant she stood up and walked to the front of the room.

I looked at Tony. He glanced from one to the other of his buddies, smiling in pride and triumph. His girl, the smile proclaimed, wouldn't back off from telling her story.

"Hi, my name's Anne and I'm an alcoholic," she said in a hollow, mechanical voice. "I'm here to talk about . . ." Her gaze slid over to Tony. He was staring at her, leaning forward—elbows on the table, fists under his chin.

Was she going to give in to Tony and talk about things she'd done while she was drinking? I closed my eyes, I didn't want to hear it. When I opened them again, Anne was looking straight at me.

She cleared her throat. When she began speaking again, her voice sounded more natural. "I'm here to talk about what my life has been and how it's going to change," she said firmly. "For one," she went on, "I know I'd have a better job right now if I hadn't . . . if there weren't too many times when I'd shown up for work with a hangover."

She wasn't going into details. I gave her a thumbs-up sign. She caught my eye but then looked away, her gaze fluttering toward Tony.

"If I hadn't been drinking, I wouldn't have had all those fights with my mother." She was looking straight ahead now, at her audience. "Also, there wouldn't be so many bills—bills that will take me a long time to pay."

Tony now sat back, arms crossed in front of his chest. Anne had disappointed him—no lurid details. A few others in the audience stirred restively. This was not the usual speech.

"It's easy to sum up," Anne said, forcing a little laugh. "Alcohol has caused a lot of problems for me, I guess we all know about the problems."

"You tell 'em, sister," a man's voice shouted from the back of the room.

"I didn't get up here to talk about my problems," Anne went on. She was speaking quickly now, the words tumbling out. "I know you're never supposed to say you've got the drinking problem licked—but I feel so good. I have an announcement. I want everyone to know that today is my six-month birthday. I haven't had a drink in six months."

There was a round of applause, another shout from the back of the room. "You keep coming to A.A. meetings, baby!"

Anne's eyes were riveted on Tony. He abruptly started a conversation with one of the men beside him. Their voices were only nominally quiet—Anne would have to speak more loudly if she were to continue to be heard.

Anne stared at Tony in hurt surprise, then looked resolutely away. "Being with A.A. has helped," she said, loudly. "It's a real help, but that's not all there is."

Tony's conversation with his buddy lapsed into silence. He'd made his hands into fists, and was drumming them on the table.

"I just want to say one more thing," Anne went on hurriedly. "I'm so grateful for the help I've gotten from everyone. And . . . thank you for listening to me tonight."

With that, she ducked her head and scuttled back to our table.

"Anne!" I squeezed her hand. "That was wonderful!"

"I meant every word," she said, smiling at last.

We waited out the rest of the meeting. Afterward, a small group came to Anne, crowding around her with congratulations. Someone suggested getting up a group to go to an ice cream parlor and celebrate.

"Do you want to go?" I asked Anne.

"No," she said. "Tony and I were supposed to . . ." She broke off, gazing around in alarm. "Where's Tony?"

He'd disappeared altogether. No one seemed to know where he was or when he'd left.

$\triangledown$

3 2

T HE NEXT NIGHT, THURSDAY, Mueller's seminar was scheduled at the Tolversons'. Vince and I had agreed to a schedule of our own—a twilight visit to Ione.

"What did you learn about the Muellers when you checked with the Bakersfield police?" I asked when he arrived.

"I think they got out before the heat was on—I didn't learn nothing from the Bakersfield police. But I called the Better Business Bureau down there. They'd had some inquiries about his investment stuff. Maybe the Muellers knew they had a couple of suspicious customers on their hands. They probably got a good instinct for when it's time to pull up stakes."

We left when the sun was low in the sky, in Vince's Chevy. We arrived in Ione just after sunset; I directed him along the country roads leading to the Muellers' place.

"No Taurus parked in the carport," I observed. "They must have taken both cars."

"Odd," Vince said.

"Well, they're gone for sure." I motioned to a light illuminating the yard, shining dully in the remaining daylight. "They wouldn't turn on the yard light before dark unless they were leaving."

"Let's check the house first," Vince said.

We stood on the wooden steps in front of the door, listening intently. Silence. Vince slowly turned the knob. "Locked," he whispered.

He shone his flashlight underneath the mobile home. "Grass still growing." He chuckled. "Bet they don't let grass grow under their feet for long." He poked me in the arm, chortling. "Get it?"

"I'm afraid so." I led the way around toward the rear of the mobile home.

We shone our flashlights into windows here and there, but could see virtually nothing, except the one large window gave us a view of what seemed to be a combination living-dining area. A small typewriter and several neat stacks of paper were on the dining table. The room contained nothing else but ordinary household things.

We headed for the barn. The double doors were half-open; we stood silently outside for a moment, then stepped in for a look at the dim interior. A disused-seeming workbench extended along one wall. Vince played his flashlight along it. "Nothing recent—except maybe that can of car polish and the rags with it."

Vince and I both jumped, startled by a sudden sound.

"Refrigerator motor," I said. I motioned toward the back wall. Vince aimed his flashlight; I'd been right. He moved the flashlight's beam along the far wall, illuminating an interior door.

I started for it; he grabbed my arm. The meaning of the look he gave me was plain. *Emma, let me take care of it.*

I shrugged off his hold. "Vince, there's no one here." I opened the door and swung it wide.

We shone our lights on an unmade bed, at the foot of it an overflowing ash tray and a beer can sitting on the floor—Hooper's living quarters, I was certain. The only other furniture was a dresser, the top drawer open crookedly and a sock dangling down. Hooks along the wall held several empty coathangers, and a ratty-looking down vest. More of Hooper's possessions were in two cardboard cartons stacked in the corner, and strewn on the floor.

"There won't be anything here," I said.

"Right," Vince agreed. "That Hooper sure ain't much of a housekeeper. Now me, I like to keep things tidy."

I was in no mood for a pitch from Vince about his desirable traits. "The stuff we want has got to be in that upstairs workroom," I said.

We went back outside and climbed the stairs, then paused on the small landing at the top. Off to one side was a small window with double-hung sash, its panes reflecting the last rosy glimmer of daylight. In front of us was a brand-new door, tightly closed. And locked—a padlock hung in the hasp.

"Uh-oh," Vince muttered. He eyed the window.

It was off to one side of the landing. Probably, with Vince hanging onto me to give some support, I could lean across and play a few tricks to get it open. The idea had no appeal.

I tried the padlock. It was in place, but not snapped shut. I swung the door open wide, then grinned at Vince. "Hooper's doing, maybe."

The room was a scramble of mis-matched office furniture and computer equipment. Cartons were stacked everywhere—some opened, brochures spilling out. A large work table was in the middle of the room, somewhat in the style of the Jobs First office.

I closed the door behind us, and snapped on the lights. "Let's have a look at the literature first," I said.

There was a surprising variety: a *Strong America Fund* brochure I'd seen at Frannie's, scattered copies of *Strong America Financial Newsletter*, a neat stack of *Christian Unity Quarterly*, faded copies of *Survival: A Magazine for the Next Millennium*, and a box labeled *ODF Research Reports*.

"What do you suppose ODF is?" Vince asked.

I looked inside the box. "Organization for Democracy and the Family."

"Family," Vince quipped. "Sure, the Mueller family."

He busied himself collecting samples of the brochures; I moved on to the computer work station and began looking through the materials stacked there. On top was a file folder labeled *CUQ–Dec.* A future issue of *Christian Unity Quarterly?* It was full of old clippings from newspapers and what seemed to be rough drafts of articles.

The title of one of the typewritten drafts caught my eye. *Child Abuse False Alarms: More Than Half of All Cases Unsubstantiated, Survey Shows.*

Now what kind of malarky was this?

> *A U.S. House of Representatives select committee has released results of a fifty-state survey, at last shedding the light of common sense on this country's recent and foolish epidemic of alarm over so-called child abuse. The report shows that child abuse—or even neglect— occurred in only forty-four per cent of the cases reported.*
>
> *"The sanctity of the family has too long been abrogated, and this is but one of the outrageous intrusions foisted by government on the besieged American Family," said Christian Unity Council Executive Director Carl Mueller.*

The articles in the folder were numbered, the numbers written in green felt tip pen; the news clippings had matching numbers. The phoney piece on child abuse statistics went on with a yellowed AP report out of Washington.

> *Shaky Child-Abuse Reports Criticized:*
> *Unsubstantiated reports of child abuse and neglect are robbing public agencies of resources to serve children in real danger, a child-abuse expert has reported to a House Committee. Investigating such reports, according to the research scholar, "eats up precious resources that could be better used to protect children who are in real and obvious danger."*

"Rats!" I said.

"What you got?" Vince asked.

"Plenty of malarky—but nothing we can use to prove the Muellers are operating a scam."

"It's okay." Vince grinned, waving a sheaf of brochures. "I got six different pitches here—with forms on the back to send in your money. All we got to do now is follow up on the bank accounts and prove they didn't use the money like they said they would." He picked through his sheaf of brochures. "Here. Here's a set for you."

I thought about that. *We.* "Why do *we* have to prove they pocketed the money? Why not just turn a set of the brochures over to the police?—tell them the story and let them do the work?"

Vince looked crestfallen. "I suppose you're right. I can take that stuff tonight to Bunco and Theft in Sacramento."

Good enough—*finis* to *Chizzit and Valenti, Investigators.*

We turned off the light, put the padlock back the way it had been, and started down the stairs. "Not bad," I said to Vince with some satisfaction. "We didn't even have to break and enter."

He ignored that point. "When I get down to the station," he said, "I got to talk to that detective, too—Laughlin. They need their tails twisted about doing something to catch the guy that went after you."

"And killed Esther Vajic," I reminded him.

"Yeah." He took hold of my arm, turning me toward him. Then he put a ham-sized hand on each of my shoulders. Now look, Emma, I got to go back to Fairville tonight, but I'm coming back to be at that art show." His blue eyes gazed earnestly into mine. "You can count on me. I'm gonna be there all weekend. I got the days off—Friday, Saturday, and Sunday."

Old Lonely. *Semper fidelis.* Three days—I was beginning to feel as if he'd installed himself in my life permanently.

$\triangledown$

3 3

VINCE HAD INSISTED ON treating me to pie and coffee before he left for Fairville; it was late when he left me off in front of the house. As I walked up the driveway, I noticed there was no familiar flickering of television light in Frannie's den—not that Frannie wasn't home, because the kitchen lights were on. I wondered if something had happened to upset her. If so, she was probably sitting in her breakfast nook and doing some serious eating.

Curious to know if something out of the way had happened at the seminar, I phoned the Tolversons.

I apologized for the lateness of the hour.

"Oh, but I'm glad you called," Elmer Tolverson said. "Me and the missus, we was real worried. And we was just talking about calling you—even with it being so late and all."

"What happened at the meeting?"

"That fourflusher Mueller! The man's crookeder than a dog's hind leg."

My feelings exactly.

"So what happened when the Muellers put on their pitch?"

"It didn't go so good from the start. Mrs. Mueller wasn't there, you know. By golly, she must be half the steam in that locomotive. He was really off his speed."

Madame Chignon hadn't been there. Of course—the Taurus wouldn't have been missing from the carport unless she'd gone somewhere separately. Out recruiting for her *brigade*, most likely.

"I challenged Mueller," Elmer Tolverson said, "caught him a couple of times on the facts."

"A friend of mine and I have been checking into him—we found out plenty," I said. "My friend is taking some information to the Bunco and Theft squad downtown."

"I'm glad to hear it. Me and Elvira, we was worried what to do on that angle."

"How did Mueller respond when you challenged him?"

"He got huffy—went all on his dignity and said I was unpatriotic."

Rachel must have known her husband might flub the presentation without her. *Sweetheart* and *Cupcake* were a team act. Her absence was a real puzzle—unless she'd somehow got wind he was keeping money from her.

"What happened after Mueller accused you of being unpatriotic?" I asked.

"Oh, my golly! That just put the monkey wrench into everything! Frannie jumped up to defend me. I don't think I ever seen a woman so discombobulated."

I could well imagine.

"Frannie left right after Mueller did," Elmer said. "We couldn't stop her from going home all upset—Elvira sure tried."

"Good for Elvira," I said. "I'll keep you posted."

I tucked a sampling of the Muellers' send-money brochures into my jacket pocket, not being sure whether I'd need to deliver a coup de grace to Frannie's faith in their scams. Then, reluctantly, I descended my stairs and went to knock on Frannie's kitchen door.

"Frannie, it's me, Emma."

"Oh, my!" I could hear her scuttling around the kitchen, a sound of something being put into the sink—Frannie's sensitive about anyone knowing she indulges in late-hour eating sessions.

She opened the door. "For Heaven's sake! Come in, Emma." She'd managed to put on a smile, but her eyes were red-rimmed and most of her makeup was rubbed away. "What brings you out so late?"

"I saw your light," I said.

"Oh. Well. Come in."

"Okay, for a little bit." She was putting up quite a front. I debated the wisdom of maneuvering her into a conversation about tonight's seminar.

Frannie moved quickly into the kitchen. "I was just about to have some ice cream. Would you like some?"

I'd followed her into the kitchen. She shooed me toward the breakfast nook and away from the sink, which, I was sure, contained a spoon and a large bowl—evidence she'd already been at the ice cream.

"Sit down," she said, and hurried to the refrigerator.

"Remember that yummy *pistachio deluxe* we had the other night?" She smiled brightly, pulling out the carton from the freezer compartment. It was the half-gallon size— and didn't seem to me as if there were much left in it.

Frannie looked at the ice cream carton as if surprised at its lack of heft. Then she rummaged in the refrigerator and pulled out a canister of whipping cream and a jar of maraschino cherries.

Her bright smile was again in place. "Let's see, how about a special treat—pistachio parfait?"

"Sure." I shifted uneasily in my seat, adjusting my jacket to make sure the brochures stayed hidden. "Do you want me to get down the parfait glasses?"

"No, no. I'll do it." Frannie dragged the kitchen stool across the floor.

It seemed to me that neither Carl nor Rachel posed any further threat to Frannie's bank account. They'd be too busy pulling up stakes—either as a team or separately. Good-bye *Sweetheart*. Good-bye *Cupcake*.

Frannie spooned what remained of the ice cream into tall slender glasses, carefully conserving the scanty supply by not squishing it down. She filled the empty places with whipped cream, then topped each serving with a cherry.

I wouldn't confront her about her misplaced faith in the Muellers—no more than I'd let on I knew about her eating sessions. Frannie was entitled to her pride.

"I'm glad you came down for a visit," she said when she brought the tall, elegant-looking parfaits to the table.

I said I was, too. I meant it.

$\triangledown$

34

THE NEXT MORNING—FRIDAY—I STOOD at my kitchen window, first cup of coffee in hand, and stared glumly at Frannie's porte cochere. Vince's old Chevy was parked there.

I wondered what time he'd gotten up this morning. He'd planned to go home to Fairville last night; it must have been after midnight before he'd arrived there—he'd have to have spent some time at the Sacramento police station after he left me off. I couldn't imagine why he was here so early.

Frannie's house was still buttoned up, the kitchen curtains closed. Vince sat behind the wheel of the Chevy, which looked more faded and dusty than ever, reading a newspaper. As I watched, he glanced up and saw me. A big smile creased his face. He waved.

I waved back. For an instant I felt almost sentimental about Old Lonely as I watched him thrust the newspaper aside, struggle out of the car, and lumber eagerly toward my stairs. But the thought that I would have him on my hands for three entire days evaporated my sentimentality.

I invited Vince in with as much grace as I could muster, and offered him a cup of coffee.

He seated himself at my kitchen table, seeming to take up a great deal of space. He yawned prodigiously.

"I wish you'd get a little more sleep," I said tartly.

"Huh? Oh—no trouble coming back here this early. I got to thinking. Maybe if I didn't show up early, you'd be off somewheres and I wouldn't get to come along and help."

"Very thoughtful of you."

Sarcasm doesn't register with Vince. He smiled, looking pleased.

I poured coffee into the biggest mug I owned and set it in front of him.

"Thanks." He slurped noisily, then held the mug up as if toasting me. "This sure hits the spot. Say, you gonna help the Job First ladies today?—with that Wonderful Women thing?"

I admitted I was. "Women Working Wonders," I corrected him.

"I could be real helpful. I could check out the security for you—with all the nut cases around, you got to be real careful. Don't forget, the Sacramento Stalker hasn't been caught yet."

I didn't want to think about the Stalker. But it was odd—he hadn't attacked anyone else. There'd been no news of him since the flap about revealing his identifying characteristic.

"I'm gonna check back with the Sacramento department today," Vince said. "I'll look up that Laughlin guy, too, and see what gives." He took a long pull at his coffee, and set the mug out for me to refill. "But first I'll help your ladies."

"They'll be glad for some extra help," I said. "It's been a squeaker, getting everything ready in time."

Vince gave me one of his ear-to-ear grins, then ducked his head and self-consciously ran his hands through his hair.

It was combed straight back—he'd apparently wet it with some kind of slick-em. He'd looked just fine before, but now the dried, stiff strands stuck out at strange angles. I had an impulse to whip out a comb, as mothers of little boys do, and put his hair to rights.

"You had breakfast yet?" Vince asked.

I told him I hadn't.

"I got a dozen eggs in the car." He got to his feet. "I'll be right back."

I fixed a three-egg breakfast for Vince, and a plentiful supply of toast, while he regaled me with the details of his visit last night to Sacramento's police department.

"I got to talk to the honcho in charge of Bunco and Theft," he said. "Otherwise they might let this drag on over the weekend with nothing getting started. By Monday the Muellers could be long gone." He ladled honey onto a half-piece of toast, folded it, and put the whole thing in his mouth. "And we got to make sure Frannie is protected," he said, talking around the mouthful of toast. "We don't want them getting more money out of her. The other thing they might do is come back and make one last grand slam pitch before they head out of town."

"I think our worries about Frannie are over," I said. I filled him in on what I had learned from Tolversons, and my visit with Frannie in her kitchen last night—everything but the amount of *pistachio deluxe* I thought she'd eaten.

"Even if Frannie's safe," Vince said, wiping his plate with the last piece of toast, "I got to make sure they get on it. Those two are gonna pull up stakes, the same as they done in Bakersfield."

He was undoubtedly right. But I wondered if Madame Chignon might try on her own to squeeze a few more dollars out of Frannie. After all, she'd been flying solo last night, somewhere. She was smart enough to figure out that her so-called crusade to rescue children might not have been discredited in Frannie's eyes. Or she might even make a pitch with a sob story about how she'd been betrayed by her husband—if she'd found out about the bank accounts. Frannie'd be a pushover for that.

"Why don't you go down to the police station first thing?" I suggested. "Afterward you can come to Lois's gallery in Old Sacramento. It'll probably take a while to get organized and lay out everything that has to be done today—there's no sense you waiting around while that happens."

"Good idea," Vince said.

"It's Muldoon Galleries, on Second Street." He took out his notebook and wrote it down.

After Vince left, I hurriedly stacked the breakfast dishes in the sink. We'd agreed on an eight o'clock planning session; I had only a few minutes to get there.

I parked in the all-day lot under the I-5 freeway, and hot-footed it to Second Street.

Muldoon Galleries occupied a classic two-story nineteenth century commercial building—narrow and deep, one of a set of three with identical fronts. The bricks had been sandblasted clean of a century's worth of paint and grime, the iron pilasters on the fronts restored to pristine conditions and freshly painted in tasteful pastels.

The tall double doors at the front of the gallery stood open. Inside, Lois and Anne were going over some papers spread on the sales counter at the rear. Brenda stood nearby, clipboard in hand and a telephone cradled to her ear. She waved me in.

"Emma," Lois crooned, "I'm so glad you're here. We really need your help." She jumped up to get an extra folding chair.

"What happened with Tony?" I whispered to Anne.

"Nothing. He hasn't come back yet." She shrugged, indicating she wasn't all that concerned. I wondered if she was putting up a front, or if he really was losing his hold on her.

"Okay," Brenda said into the phone. "Tell the people at Theodore Judah School we'll pick that stuff up at noon—oh, and stop by the Post Office on your way over, will you?" She hung up. "That was Kitty. She'll be here in a few minutes. Then we can parcel out the remaining jobs."

I asked about Coretta.

"She said last night she'd come today and help out," Lois said. "She planned to be here for the meeting, but I wouldn't call her for the world. She's been so . . . torn up. I know her doctor prescribed medication. If she's managing to get in a few hours' sleep—"

"We can manage without her," Brenda said. She consulted her clipboard. "Everything has to get checked into the gallery and put on display today." She launched into an explanation of the plan she and Lois had worked out.

I was impressed with what they'd managed to accomplish

in one week. A collection of photographs of women at work, borrowed from the Sacramento History Center, would go on the second floor, along with the Dorothea Lange collection from U.C. Davis. There'd also be photographs of women working that had been a project of one of the classes Esther Vajic had taught. The staircase rail would be decorated with schoolchildren's art—lifesize cutouts of themselves as women at work. The downstairs was reserved for exhibits from various professional organizations and trade unions.

Lois was to stay at the gallery all day, the rest of us to come and go as needed to collect materials.

"Except," Brenda said, "I'll be at the Jobs First office for a couple of phone sessions. I've got to get in last-minute-reminder calls to all the reporters."

She almost seemed to think the news coverage was more important than the event itself. Maybe she was right.

"If you talk to any news people," Brenda said, "be sure to give them our post office box number—we want mail-in contributions in Esther's memory. And, oh yes, we'll have a spot for collecting donations here at the gallery. It'll make a good visual for television." She grinned. "And it'll go as near the front door as I can manage."

"Where do we put Jonathan Lee?" Lois asked.

"No problem. He's agreed to be a roving reporter. He can stash his personal things in the storage room off the mezzanine, just like the rest of us." She turned to Anne and me. "No need to worry about our purses or other stuff getting ripped off—there's a row of storage compartments back there. Lois and I have put some padlocks on each one—just keep track of your key."

"With Benny Podesta still on the loose," Lois said, "I wish we had the funds to hire a security guard."

"I don't think we've got too much to worry about," Brenda told her. "Kitty and I talked with the police about the event this weekend—with that Detective Miller we took the letters to. He thinks Benny's going to lay low. That beaky nose is distinctive, so he doesn't think Benny would chance showing his face. But they'll sort of keep an eye out down here anyhow."

"On top on that," I announced. "We've got a security guard—a genuine off-duty policeman, free of charge for the entire weekend." I told them about Vince.

"Oh, that's splendid," Lois crooned.

"Great!" Brenda agreed, gathering up a stack of papers and her clipboard. "Well, our plans for the day are set. I've got to leave—oh, yes, if Coretta doesn't show up soon, somebody else will have to pick up the schoolkids' stuff."

As soon as Brenda had left, Lois turned to me. "How wonderful!" she exclaimed. "Your friend Vince—he'll be so helpful. I'm just delighted he'll be here." She gave me a coy look. "I'm eager to meet him."

Another *romantic*—Lord help me if she and Frannie ever got together.

Half an hour later Coretta still hadn't shown up.

"Anne, dear," Lois said. "I truly don't want to bother Coretta. Would you go over to Theodore Judah School on your way to work and pick up the children's artwork?"

"Sure thing," Anne said. "It's only a couple of blocks out of my way. I can bring them in on my lunch break."

Anne left.

"Are there some other errands that need running?" I asked.

"Brenda had a list," Lois said. She began rummaging through a stack of papers on the counter. "Here." She handed me Brenda's list. "Better stop at E-Z Rentals first, they'll be awfully busy later—everybody wants to pick up rentals on Friday afternoon."

"Heigh ho!" Kitty announced from the front door. "Mail call."

She waved a pair of envelopes and flashed a smile. But the smile didn't match the scared look on her face.

35

"WHERE'S BRENDA?" KITTY ASKED.

"She's gone over to the Jobs First office to make phone calls," Lois said. "Are those letters from . . . ?"

"Yep."

More threatening letters. And meanwhile Brenda was at the office—breaking her own rule about working there alone.

Kitty took the letters out of their envelopes and sat them side by side on the counter. One was typewritten, the other handwritten, or, more precisely, hand printed, in block letters—bold and dramatic, backslanted.

"I don't know why the last one's handwritten and without the extra stuff at the top and the bottom," Kitty said, "but it's obviously from the same person."

Obviously. Both were addressed "To the Harlots."

"The handwritten one was postmarked yesterday," Kitty added. "The other was mailed the day before."

Lois picked up the typewritten letter and began studying it. She drew her breath in sharply.

"Read it aloud," I said.

" 'I am the Alpha and the Omega, the beginning and the end,' " she read, her face pale. " 'I am fire and ice. I am night and day, he and she. I am death's chill, and the fire of the innermost circle of Hell. I am the spirit. I blow the fire of retribution upon you.' " She was shaking her head slowly from side to side as she read, as if to deny the words. " 'You must know my power,' " she continued in a whisper. " 'You must know the wind of retribution that shall scatter you all as chaff.' " She put the letter back on the table quickly, as if she could no longer bear to touch it.

"Retribution," she whispered.

I pulled the typewritten letter toward me. Across the top were all the same quotes from Revelation as in the first two letters—it was the quotes at the bottom that changed each time.

"Frightening . . . completely delusional," Lois murmured.

There were two quotes at the bottom of the letter she had just read. One was from Malachi: *"Then you will go trample down the wicked; they will be ashes under the soles of your feet."* The other was from Exodus: *"Do not allow a sorceress to live."*

"Kitty, you read the second letter," Lois said.

"It's worse. But at least it's short." She picked up the letter and read it rapidly.

"To the harlots: You will not see me when I come. The hour of your destruction is upon you. I bring terror and woe, and I shall now descend upon *all* of you."

I waited. "That's it?" I asked.

Kitty nodded.

She and Lois and I stared at each other.

"The *all* is underlined," Kitty said. "Retribution will now descend upon all of us."

36

KITTY HURRIED OFF TO take the letters to Detective Miller. "I'll ask for a stepped-up watch on the gallery this weekend," she promised.

Vince arrived almost immediately after that, and at the same time, the delivery truck with the display stands.

Lois greeted Vince effusively, telling him how wonderful she thought it was that I had a friend who was willing to help. He blushed, basking in the attention from her; she rolled *matchmaker* eyes in my direction. They deserved each other's company for a while, I thought. I took my list of errands and left.

I picked up a stack of folding chairs and two tables at E-Z Rentals, and then worked my way through the rest of the stops on the list. But I didn't go back to the gallery right away. Instead, I headed home, anticipating some lunch and a little solitude—a chance to think.

I'd scarcely pulled into the garage when Frannie scurried out.

"Oh! I'm so glad I caught you, Emma. I just can't wait to tell about my surprise."

Her face was moist with perspiration. She wore an apron and smelled faintly of vanilla.

What now?

"It's a surprise for your ladies," Frannie said, "for the fundraising event you're having this weekend." She gave me a sidelong look and smiled her best twinkly smile. She shook a finger in playful admonition. "If I know anything about fundraising," she said, "it's that you always have to have cookies to sell."

She launched into the details of the cookies she planned to bake. This was her way of apologizing, I realized, for being wrong about the Muellers. But my squabble with Frannie now seemed trivial and remote. I couldn't get my mind off the letters that Kitty had brought this morning.

I shall now descend upon all of you.

". . . already finished the chocolate delights. And I think I'll do macaroons next, and some *lebkuchen*—Emma, you're not listening to me!"

"Sorry, I was thinking about something else." I put on the best smile I could. "That's a wonderful idea, Frannie—very generous of you." I'd sounded indifferent, I knew it, and tried to put a little more enthusiasm into my voice. "I'm sure everyone will be pleased."

"Of course they'll be pleased. Gracious! Just wait until you see how much money this brings in. And I'll be there tomorrow to help with the selling."

Frannie was certainly going the extra mile. I thanked her with genuine enthusiasm, and started up my steps.

"Wait until Sunday," she called after me. "I'll have a surprise that's even more special."

"That's really great, Frannie," I responded. "You're a peach." She beamed with pleasure, and hurried back to her kitchen.

Sourpuss was waiting at the top of the steps. He twined around my ankles as I unlocked the door, and *meowed* accusingly in his gritty voice. What with feeding Vince this morning, I'd forgotten to feed him. "Come on, old boy," I said, letting us both in.

My telephone light was blinking, but I took time to put food in Sourpuss's dish before I checked the message.

It was from Lieutenant Laughlin, and his voice on the tape

sounded far livelier than when I'd talked with him at the
police station. He wanted me to call back as soon as possible.

He sounded even more upbeat when I returned the call.
"Oh, yes—glad you called. There's good news, Mrs. Chizzit.
I'm happy to inform you that we're holding a man named
Anthony Viera. We have reason to believe he may be the
Sacramento Stalker."

The Stalker. I was too astonished to say anything.

"You'll have to come down here to identify him,"
Laughlin went on, "a matter of routine."

I didn't think any identification I could make would be of
much use. I told Laughlin so. "How did you catch the man?"
I asked.

"In the course of our investigation," he said, "we checked
emergency room admissions for treatment of wounds to the
head or face." I caught a note of pride in his voice, it must
have been his idea. "We turned up this fellow, an indigent.
He was admitted Sunday to the med center over on Stockton
Boulevard—facial lacerations and a broken nose, badly infected. He waited before he got help." A chuckle. "He's a
mess. You must have really clobbered him with that flashlight."

An indigent, I thought—a common bum, just as I'd first
thought. I stared blankly at Sourpuss, who sat beside his
food dish. His mouth was open, his pink tongue licking tidily
at its edges. An *indigent*. A shiftless bum. Why would such
a man go directly from an accidental murder to a second
attempt at rape?

"We'd like you to come down and make that identification
promptly, Mrs. Chizzit," Laughlin said, sounding altogether
smug. "You know, tie up all the loose ends."

"Sure . . . sure thing." Sourpuss, with great dignity, began
licking his fur.

"This afternoon, if at all possible," Laughlin went on
smoothly, "and thank you, Mrs. Chizzit."

It was some other cat!

"Wait!" I shouted into the phone.

Some other cat, I thought, a shadow killer pretending to

be the Sacramento Stalker. *I shall now descend upon all of you.*

"This man Viera," I asked. "Did he smell of gasoline?"

"Sure." Laughlin sounded impatient.

"He smelled the way I described? As if he'd been sleeping in an old garage?"

"Yes."

"And Esther Vajic's body?" I asked.

"Um . . . well, not quite the same."

"You mean the smell was different," I said.

"The smell was faint, but it was fresh gasoline," he admitted.

I fought to keep my voice calm. "I think someone's out to get all the members of a group I belong to—Jobs First. We've been getting a series of threatening letters." I stopped, struck by the thought of Coretta's failure to appear. "There may have been another attack already," I said urgently. As I talked I reached for the phone book to look up her address. "One of us didn't show up for a meeting this morning. Her name's Coretta Vajic—she's Esther Vajic's mother."

I gave the address to Laughlin; he immediately repeated it to someone else. "We'll get right out there." The line went dead. My hand trembled as I hung up the phone.

Coretta lived on South Land Park Drive—less than ten minutes away. I hurried to my truck and backed out of the driveway, tires squealing.

I drove through the prosperous south area neighborhoods, slowing impatiently from time to time to check house numbers, which were in ascending order as I drove out on South Land Park Drive. Her address was in the 6000 block, which turned out to be further away than I'd thought. I should have taken the freeway for part of the distance, I realized.

Finally, up ahead, I saw a squad car—lights flashing—and the inevitable knot of curious onlookers gathered on the sidewalk. An officer stood by the open car door, talking on the police radio. Another was stringing crime-scene tape across the driveway.

$\triangledown$

37

MY WORST FEARS WEREN'T realized; Coretta Vajic was still alive.

Both Lieutenant Laughlin and an ambulance arrived at her house shortly after I did. I waited, watching, while the ambulance attendants hurried to the back of the house with their gurney, and then emerged with Coretta, unconscious and bundled in a blanket.

After the ambulance left, Laughlin and I stood in the driveway, talking. The officers had found her on the patio at the rear of the house, he told me.

"It was more or less the same thing that happened with the daughter. She was apparently approached from behind, struck on the head, and the instrument left at the scene—a crescent wrench this time, the officers found it on the lawn."

"And the smell of gasoline?"

He nodded. "The smell already was faint—it was dabbed onto her clothing, as near as I could tell." He stared abstract-edly at the last few curious onlookers who still stood on the front sidewalk. "She was in her bathrobe," he went on. "It was pulled off her shoulders a bit, to make it seem like another attempted rape." His hands went to his scalp, he began scratching both sides at the same time, just above the ears. "Clumsy—I don't know why I didn't see it before. Except that

170

with the daughter, the red jumpsuit . . . it looked more . . ."

I waited. He didn't finish the sentence. More like a *scarlet woman*, I thought.

Laughlin seemed to be trying to absorb the lesson for future reference. "Um . . ." he said, and lapsed into silence again.

I asked if he knew when Coretta had been attacked.

"This morning, most likely. She was using the garden hose, apparently to hand-water some plants on the patio. The hose was still running—water accumulating—but not so much that it would have been collecting since last night." He turned back, glanced abstractedly toward the back of the house, and then started us moving toward the sidewalk.

"There's a Detective Miller who has all those threatening letters we've received. Do you know him?"

"Miller . . . um . . . yeah, I do."

"The letters promised retribution. The letter writer said now he would descend upon all of us."

"You think it's the same person?"

"Yes. Definitely."

He stared off into the distance. "Tell me why."

It rankled, I thought, his missing the difference in smell. "Here's what I think," I said. "The television stations didn't report about a gasoline smell being the Stalker's identifying characteristic until Saturday. But Esther was killed Friday."

"So we didn't think about a copycat," Laughlin said glumly. "The heat's on about finding the Stalker, so we ignore the improbability of a rape attempt and a murder at nearly the same time, and we miss a difference in the description of a smell." He started scratching his head.

"Don't be hard on yourself," I said. "I bought into it too, about the guy killing Esther and then coming after me—even though I thought it was strange, I bought it."

Laughlin's head scratching became more fierce. "I shouldn't have missed it," he said disconsolately.

"I still think you're being too hard on yourself," I said, wondering how much more torture his scalp could stand. "A killer trying to operate in the Stalker's shadow, would have to be someone who heard one of the KXPR broadcasts on

Thursday or Friday."

"Yeah. Most of our clientele don't listen to stuff like that."

"I suppose not," I said. Whoever killed Esther and attacked Coretta was probably sending those letters, I thought,
but it still didn't make sense. Would that kind of person be
listening to a liberal . . . *egghead* . . . radio station?

"Will you be talking with Detective Miller about those
letters?"

He sighed. "Yeah. We'll see what we can turn up." He
gestured in the direction the ambulance had taken. "You
going to follow her to the hospital?"

"Yes."

"You know her next of kin?"

I hadn't thought about that. "I'll make some phone calls
from the hospital waiting room," I said. "Maybe one of the
Jobs First members knows about her family."

At the hospital I had a long wait—and couldn't learn
much. Coretta was still unconscious, they wouldn't know
whether she'd be okay until she was awake and coherent. I
made notes of what I was told, that there was a concussion
and probably a blood clot—a sub-dural hematoma. There
wouldn't be much more to know until they'd done a scan,
and probably surgery after that.

I phoned the gallery to tell Lois what had happened and
asked her to break the news to the others. She told me Vince
had long since finished with the display stands and left,
saying he wanted to have a talk with the Sacramento police.
Anne was at work, and Kitty was in and out, collecting
exhibit materials. Brenda had gone back to the Jobs First
office to finish her phone calls to the news reporters.

I was concerned that Brenda was alone at the Jobs First
office, but didn't share my anxiety with Lois. "I'll bring the
folding chairs and the other stuff to the gallery later in the day,"
I said to her. "Oh, yes. Do you know anything about Coretta's
family? The police want to know about next of kin."

"Her former husband lives in Placerville."

That would be easy enough for the police to check. "I'll
call and break the news to Brenda," I told Lois, and hung up.

I phoned and left word for Laughlin about Coretta's ex-husband, and then tried to call Brenda. I got a busy signal. After suitable waits, I made a second and third try—the same thing. I decided to go to the Jobs First office.

At this time of the afternoon, parking spaces on J Street were scarce. I had to settle for a space by the corner on the opposite side of the street, near the bakery. I was putting coins in the parking meter when I heard the roar of a heavy engine in low gear. The sound was wrong somehow, I thought—not consistent with the usual truck-traffic noises.

I heard a loud crash, turned, and was astonished to see an old truck nosed into one side of the Jobs First storefront. Window glass crashed down onto the truck hood. More glass fell—slowly, the sound dominating the sudden silence. Cars still passed by, most of the drivers oblivious, a few craning their necks to see.

The truck's engine roared into life; its gears clashed. It backed away from the building, blocking the traffic lane on that side. Like the drivers of the cars, I momentarily had trouble believing what I was seeing. But then the reality of it came down on me like an avalanche.

Brenda! I forced myself to be calm. Brenda would be all right. She would have been in the back room, she'd surely run to safety in the alley.

The truck moved forward again, the engine louder than before, its heavy front aimed at the other window. It looked to me to be a vintage military truck, perhaps even from World War II. I'd seen trucks like that in the old wartime newsreels—the backs canvas-covered, filled with men who stared out with anxious eyes.

I heard a terrible wrenching sound as the front of the truck again connected with the building. It had hit the remaining window at one edge. The glass hung crazily in large pieces, then began crashing in chunks onto the sidewalk.

By this time traffic had stopped and cars blocked the lanes. People emerged from offices and stores on both sides of the street. The crowd grew rapidly, filled with a buzz of murmurs and low exclamations, watching as if transfixed.

A man, in white shirt and pants, who'd come out from the bakery stood beside me. I grabbed his arm. "Call the cops!"

He stared at me.

"Go back inside," I shouted. "Use your phone—call the police!"

He turned and hurried inside.

The truck's engine revved, its gears ground, but it didn't move—apparently the driver was having trouble getting the old transmission into reverse. The gears meshed; the truck lurched backward.

The driver pulled it sharply to one side. I watched, puzzled, until I realized he was maneuvering to get into position to attack the building from a different angle.

I saw his face.

I was certain it was Benny Podesta—prominent nose, swarthy complexion.

He looked up, appearing to notice the crowd for the first time. He grinned and waved a fist, as if expecting approval, and shouted something I couldn't make out.

No one responded, except the people nearest the truck; they moved back uneasily. It seemed to me the crowd stayed behind an invisible boundary. No one would cross the line, but everyone pressed close, eager to see and hear as much as possible, as if Benny Podesta and his truck were nothing more than a scene from a new and fascinating action-adventure television program.

Podesta again shouted—something unintelligible—and went back to clashing the truck's gears.

Had the man from the bakery called the police?

I looked. He was on the phone, gesticulating wildly. The downtown police station was scarcely ten blocks from us. How long before they got here?

Podesta had the truck in gear again and moved it forward slowly—aiming carefully, directly toward the center of the storefront and the office door. The truck edged forward at a snail's pace and then touched the office entry.

Where were the police?

The noise of the truck motor began a steadily ascending

crescendo. At the same time Podesta ducked momentarily out of sight in the truck's cab. The crowd edged forward, then recoiled suddenly as the truck door opened. Podesta was squeezing out of the partly-open truck door, avoiding the glass shards held in place by the frame of the smashed window. The building shuddered. The truck's motor was still running; I realized he must have tied down the accelerator.

The engine died.

Podesta strode away from the truck. People pushed urgently backward, shoving each other in their haste to keep their distance. He looked back once and shrugged.

Police sirens wailed.

By this time Podesta had reached the curb on the opposite side of the street, the crowd still falling back in front of him. He looked to the right and then to the left, a triumphant gesture, as if he awaited certain approval. Then he stood on tip-toe, both fists clenched high in the air.

The crowd was silent, still slowly edging away from him, looking around anxiously for the police cars.

Podesta seemed not to notice. He stuck his chin out, Mussolini-style, and began to shout. Whatever he said was loaded with obscenities, I could make out very little of it—except several times I heard "frigging women." He gestured repeatedly at the Jobs First office, each time looking around the crowd, smiling, nodding as if acknowledging encouragement.

Podesta was in a world of his own, I realized. He was a leader for a just cause, a gifted speaker exhorting an admiring audience, a preacher giving his all to a rapt congregation.

The sirens wailed closer, and wound to a stop. Officers pushed through the crowd.

Podesta still gesticulated and yelled as the officers approached him. At the last minute he started to run.

He didn't get far. Two officers wrestled him to the ground and the fight suddenly went out of him. He offered no objections as they handcuffed him and led him to one of the police cars. One of the officers put a hand on top of his head and pushed down, guiding him easily into the back seat.

$\triangledown$

3 8

Aт SEVEN O'CLOCK THAT night Brenda, Kitty, Lois, Anne, and I sat in the back room at the gallery, all of us pretty much worn out. We'd learned from the hospital that Coretta had undergone surgery and was expected to recover, and we'd gotten the worst of the mess cleaned up at the Jobs First office. Now the problem on our minds was keeping ourselves safe from *Retribution,* as we'd decided to name whoever was writing those letters.

"We'll be sitting ducks this weekend at the gallery," Kitty said glumly, "neatly lined up—all in a row."

"Not necessarily," Lois said. "Before Vince left, he and I looked over the premises. He thinks we'll be perfectly secure as long as we keep the door to the alley locked. There's a good, strong deadbolt on it."

"I'm sure Vince is right about being relatively safe at the gallery," Brenda said, "but . . ." Her voice trailed off.

I knew what she hadn't put into words. We all did. What about after we went home?

There was an uncomfortable silence.

"I keep wondering," Lois said, "if it's someone we know."

Lois's remark didn't improve the comfort level.

"It couldn't be anyone we know," Brenda said crisply. "Retribution is a religious nut. We'd know if—"

176

"Don't be too sure of that," Kitty said. "The person we're dealing with is no Benny Podesta. There's a lot of cleverness here."

"Golly," Anne said. "What if Kitty's right? What if it's somebody just hiding behind the religious stuff? After all, Retribution wanted us to think he was the Sacramento Stalker."

It didn't seem likely, but the *someone we know* possibility made me uneasy. Kitty had brought copies of the last two letters with her; they were right in front of me on the counter.

They were labeled: *Letter # 3, Rec'd 2nd Friday,* and *Letter # 4, Rec'd 2nd Friday.* One had been postmarked yesterday, Kitty had said, the other the day before.

The letter with the *now you know* message had arrived before Esther was killed. And we'd gotten the last one, the one that said *now I will descend upon all of you,* before we knew about Coretta. Retribution must have overestimated the time it would take us to receive them. Other than the timing, however, almost everything about the letters suggested careful planning and an almost compulsive attention to detail.

Except the last letter. Handwritten—an aberration.

"None of us ought to be alone at night," Brenda said. "Not until Retribution is caught."

"I'm way ahead of you, chum," Kitty responded. "I've got an aunt in Fair Oaks—I've already set it up to stay with her."

I gave Anne a *what-about-you?* look.

"Tony's away on a business trip," she said quickly.

Brenda and Kitty exchanged knowing glances.

I wondered if he had been gone since the night of the A.A. meeting. Regardless of the threat from Retribution, Anne shouldn't be alone. If Tony were on an extended binge he might come back still drunk—and violent.

"I can stay with one of my girlfriends," Anne said, raising her chin defensively. "I've done it before."

I began thinking about my own situation, I seldom keep my house closed up. No matter that I had an upstairs place—I'd lock *everything* tonight.

The phone rang. Lois answered it, and then, all smiles, handed the phone to me. "It's Vince."

Maybe he was calling from Frannie's. I'd been wondering why I hadn't heard from him.

"Emma," he said plaintively, "I been trying to get ahold of you. I was worried. Frannie's worried, too, you not being home yet."

"Are you at Frannie's? Tell her—"

"I'm in Carson City."

"What!"

"Now, don't get excited. I tailed Mueller from Ione up to here—it was the only way to know for sure where he was going."

Carson City, Nevada. Three hours from Ione—at least. "Let me get this straight, Vince. You followed Mueller?"

"Right. I figured I better have a look-see. I got up there, to Ione, drove up that road. No sign of the missus, or her car, but there they were, Mueller and the guy that works for him."

"Hooper."

"Yeah. Mueller and Hooper were loading boxes of stuff into a U-Haul trailer they had hitched to that big gray Chrysler. I didn't want them to notice me so I drove right on by. But then, up the hill, I found a spot to wait and watch."

"And you followed them all the way to Carson City?"

"Yeah. There weren't no other way to know where they were going—they'd probably give a phony address to the U-Haul people."

There was nobody like Vince for stick-to-it determination. "Congratulations," I said. "Maybe from now on I'll call you Bulldog Valenti."

"Huh?"

"You're like the Canadian Mounties—you always get your man."

"Aw . . ."

I could imagine him blushing.

"Emma, I got to get me some supper. I ain't had nothing

to eat since this morning, what with tracking Mueller around, and I had to wait hours before they had the trailer loaded. Then I'm gonna come on back to Sacramento. You tell Frannie not to wait up. Just leave the side door unlocked, okay? And you better call her."

"I'll be going home right away." Leaving the side door unlocked didn't sound like a good idea to me. We'd work something out.

"Just so Frannie knows you're all right," Vince said, "she was real anxious to know when you'd be home."

"Vince—did you tell Frannie where you were and why?"

A pause. "Yeah."

"And . . . ?"

"I didn't get the chance to spell it out for her. She . . ."

"She didn't want to hear about it?"

"She sure didn't. But she got the general idea, all right."

As soon as I'd hung up, I made quick explanations to the others about my conversation with Vince and then headed home. Frannie had her porch light on, and came out to meet me in the driveway.

"Gracious! I thought you'd never get home. Vince wanted to talk to you. He phoned you at the gallery, didn't he?"

"Yes. I'm sorry you were worried."

But Frannie didn't seem worried now, I realized. She was eager, excited.

"Come on along!" She tugged on my arm. "I've got something to show you!" She urged me into the house—all tugs and excitement. When we reached the patio room she stopped. She had the door closed.

"What's the surprise?" I asked.

She smiled, eyes gleaming, and started singing a fanfare. "Ta-da-da dah . . ." She flung open the door. ". . . ta-*dah!*"

Lined up on the coffee table were three huge Tupperware containers, circular and flat.

Frannie waltzed over to the table. "This one's the choco-late delight bars." She drummed her fingers on the top of the first container. "And, here, macaroons." More drumming. "And this . . ." She picked up the last container. "This is the *lebkuchen*—half with glazed pineapple, half with dates."

She'd really outdone herself.

"Oh! Just you wait until Sunday! There's going to be more. We're going to have something *really* special."

Frannie's eyes sparkled—her I've-got-a-secret look. There was no point in asking. I'd just have to wait until Sunday and cope with the surprise then.

I was certain there'd be no more said about where Vince had been or why he'd made the trip. I was willing to leave it at that. All's well that ends well, I thought, and no sense in ruining it with a lot of palaver.

$\triangledown$

3 9

THE NEXT MORNING VINCE was still sleeping when Frannie and I were ready to leave.

"Gracious!" she exclaimed. "I wouldn't wake him for the world!" She fussed over leaving a note in the kitchen—and orange juice, an insulated carafe of coffee, croissants, and a plate heaped with sliced cold ham and assorted cheeses. I waited impatiently.

"Where's the card table and the other stuff that has to go to the gallery?" I asked.

Frannie gestured toward the hall. Stacked beside the side door were the card table, two of the set of folding chairs that matched it, a tagboard sign and a portable sign easel—as well as the three canisters of cookies and a cardboard box. Inside the box was a folded tablecloth, several of Frannie's good platters, paper napkins, and a small cash box.

"Is your car trunk still full of those carpet and drapery samples you picked up last week?" I asked.

"Gracious! Yes, it is."

"I think we ought to take the truck," I said, knowing full well that Frannie doesn't like to ride in it. "Or you could come separately in the Mercedes."

"It's all right," Frannie said, a note of deliberate uncon-cern in her voice. Another conciliatory gesture—probably the last ramification of the business about the Muellers.

When we arrived at the gallery, I double-parked out front and Frannie and I carried in the three containers of cookies. Lois, Brenda, Kitty, and Anne were already there; Lois hurried forward to greet us. I introduced Frannie and explained about the cookies.

"How marvelous!" Lois enthused. "And I'm just delighted to meet you, Frannie. Emma has told us about her wonderful friend—well, *I* think you're wonderful. Not just for bringing the cookies to help us raise funds, but also for offering Emma's friend Vince a place to stay and all. And he's just the nicest man, don't you think?"

Frannie, basking in the attention, agreed wholeheartedly.

When Lois had mentioned Vince, she'd glanced covertly in my direction. I knew what that kind of look meant. Dear God! Two matchmakers getting together—double jeopardy.

"Where's Vince?" Lois asked coyly as Brenda came over to join us.

"He'll be here later," I said.

I saw Brenda's flicker of worry that Vince wouldn't be around for a while. The more protection the better, I supposed. We were all worried, though none of us were acknowledging it openly. I hoped Frannie would be too engrossed in her cookie sales to pick up on it.

"Where do you want to put the cookie-sale table?" I asked.

The gallery was already crowded with exhibits and display tables. Brenda had set up her money-collecting station in one of the front windows alongside the double-door entrance. The entire window space was taken up with a long narrow table, piled with leaflets about the Women Working Wonders exhibit, and supporting a tall plastic see-through tube for donations. The tube was marked in red at intervals—a goal for today, another for tomorrow. Somebody, probably Brenda, had already seeded it with a few bills.

The only available spot for selling cookies was a narrow space by the window opposite Brenda's donation set-up.

"Oh, dear!" Lois exclaimed. "I wasn't going to put anything in the other window. It gets so hot in the afternoons."

This afternoon the sun would be shining full force on that window, and Frannie didn't fare well in the heat.

"It's quite all right," she said cheerfully.

There was no other space available. I'd spell Frannie for a while this afternoon, I decided. I brought the table, chairs and the rest of the things in from the truck, then drove over to park it in the all-day lot.

The weather was already turning warm. I suspected we were beginning one of those autumn scorchers we have from time to time in Sacramento.

By the time I'd hoofed it back to the gallery from the parking lot, Frannie—all smiles—had finished setting up her cookie sales table. She bubbled with enthusiasm. "Isn't this just fabulous? Being in the window like this, people can see my sign from the street—and see the cookies, too. They won't be able to resist. Mark my words, we'll make *tons* of money!"

"I don't see how it can miss, Frannie," I said. "I'll give you some relief at the sales table when it gets hot this afternoon," I added.

"You won't have to." She flashed a twinkly smile in my direction. "Everything will be sold by then. We can go home early. Won't that be nice?"

Going home early wasn't what I'd had in mind, but I could take that up with her later. I left her happily arranging cookies on the platters and went to see how I could help out. But Brenda was talking on the phone and Lois had scurried to the front door to greet a pair of women who had just arrived. Kitty and Anne were somewhere upstairs, I could hear their voices.

I hadn't had yet had a look at the part of the gallery behind the sales counter, or the mezzanine or second floor. I decided to duplicate the security inspection Lois and Vince had done yesterday.

Immediately behind the sales counter was the open stairway to the mezzanine and upstairs, now decorated with an ascending parade of children's lifesize cutouts. The kids had pictured themselves as women doctors, astronauts, loggers, chefs, police officers—even a female scuba diver, underwater camera in hand.

Behind the sales counter was a hallway along the left-hand wall of the building. It obviously led to the back door; along it were two doors. The first, which I expected was a stairway to the basement, was closed. I tried it—locked. It still had the original square hardware, the kind that houses both doorknob and lock. And it probably could be opened with almost any kind of probe. Or a well-placed kick.

The second door, braced open with a case of empty wine bottles, led into a room equipped with a refrigerator, several tired-looking upholstered chairs and a couch. At the back end was a door marked "Rest Room." Lois had set up TV trays beside the chairs and in front of the couch. A sign was taped on the front of the refrigerator—"Help Yourself."

I went to the alley door, with its new-looking deadbolt lock, and slid back the bolt. The door opened directly onto the alley.

I squinted into the glare of morning sunshine. Up and down the alley were other back entrances to buildings, garbage cans placed alongside most of them. Two doors over, across the alley, one of the buildings sported a backyard that had been made over into a restaurant patio. It was shielded from the alley by a row of slender trees and a vine-covered high fence. All I could see of the patio was the tops of shade umbrellas, which sported ads for imported beer.

I closed and locked the door. On my way back I spotted the key to the basement entry hanging on a nail near the door. I unlocked it.

A rickety stairway led down into darkness; a light cord dangled in front of me. When I pulled the cord, light from a bare bulb, swinging from the pull on the chain, bounced about the narrow space at the bottom of the stairs. The floor was dirt, the basement walls of old brick patched here and there with somewhat newer concrete. A doorway opening was at one side of the foot-of-the-stairs area, the entrance to the basement itself—an opening into dim blackness. I craned my neck, but could see nothing more.

Lois put a hand on my shoulder; I jumped.

"Sorry, I didn't mean to startle you," she said. "You must be doing your own security inspection. Did you get the idea from Vince? I told him, there's nothing down there but dust and spider webs—I checked when I moved into the gallery. The only dangerous thing is the stairway, it seems to me, and I didn't make a fuss with the landlord about it because I don't plan to use the basement. But it looks terribly spooky, doesn't it?"

That was as close as anyone had come today to mentioning that we might have anything to worry about.

"Oh, by the way," Lois went on. "Kitty wants your help. She and Anne brought in some plastic pennants, they're going to string them up out front."

I headed up the stairs, taking a quick time-out to inspect the mezzanine storage room. But there was little to see, except a row of storage cabinets and a window admitting a blinding glare of morning light from the alley.

Upstairs, Kitty and Anne were surrounded by coils of tangled pennants and line. Several lengths of the line were spread out on the floor, the little triangular flags all lined up to point in the same direction.

"I borrowed the pennants from my friend's neighbor," Anne said. "He works for a used car dealer." She ducked her head, blushing, and feigned absorption with the business of untangling a coil of flags.

"I'm glad your friend's neighbor is generous," I said.

I didn't doubt the man had more on his mind than plastic pennants. Starting a new relationship is a tacky way to leave a bad marriage, but I supposed Anne could make worse mistakes—staying with Tony, for one.

For the next hour I alternated between hanging over the edge of the upstairs balcony to attach the pennant lines and running down to the street to anchor them. By the time I was finished, the gallery had begun to look altogether festive.

The official Women Working Wonders opening was set for eleven o'clock. By then a mobile van from Channel Ten had arrived with a two-person camera crew and one of the station's celebrity news personalities. He was to be the opening ceremony's ribbon cutter. Brenda, in seventh heaven with this publicity coup, involved herself in the television crew's setting-up activities, which took a full ten minutes. During this time a reporter and a photographer from the *Sacramento Bee* also arrived, and a reporter-photographer from the *Suttertown News*. But no Jonathan Lee.

The ribbon-cutting "photo opportunity" was over in less than a minute. People streamed into the gallery—a number of women who'd apparently come for the event, as well as a gaggle of curious tourists in shorts and T-shirts. Brenda took the lead, her television celebrity firmly in hand, and moved to the donation table. The newscaster performed for the camera again, smilingly dropping dollar bills into the plastic tube.

I noticed that Frannie's cookie table was getting a lot of attention. I wasn't surprised. After a few people had gotten their first taste, I expected word of mouth advertising, so to speak, would bring in the customers. Frannie, busily accepting money, flashed me a look of triumph.

Vince arrived shortly after the opening, apologizing repeatedly for not being there sooner. He'd taken time to stop by the police station to give the Bunco and Theft squad detailed information about the whereabouts of Mueller and his U-Haul trailer.

Jonathan Lee had shown up at about the same time as Vince, tape recorder in hand. He was being as smarmy and obnoxious as ever—more so, in fact. His prurient interest in our fears seemed to be intensified. I quelled my resentment. He was an ambitious young snot, I told myself, nothing more. And not worth my emotional energy. We *were* afraid, of course, but not in the way Lee wanted us to be—not the bunch of Alfred-Hitchcock-movie scared stupid women he was looking for.

Maybe he'd get discouraged and leave when he discovered he wasn't getting much from any of us. It seemed to me we were all doing a good job of concealing our anxiety, for which I was grateful. But fear had stayed with me since I'd read those last two letters on Friday—a leaden, waiting-for-the-other-shoe-to-drop, sense of dread.

$\triangledown$

40

JUST AS FRANNIE HAD predicted, her cookies were sold by early afternoon. She retreated to the back room and flopped on the sofa, red-faced and perspiring.

I was worried about her. "Let me get you a soda from the refrigerator."

Frannie's not big on soft drinks. She gave a negative wave of her hand. "I just want to go home."

"You ought to get some fluid in you," I said. "How about some ice water?"

She assented. "But we'll go home as soon as I drink this. Okay? I *do* have to get home."

"Pretty quick," I told her. Brenda had asked me to fasten the children's cut-out pictures more securely. The paper figures had been held in place only with strips of double-sided tape. It wasn't holding against the breeze generated by the circulating fans Lois had set up to augment the building's feeble air conditioning.

I waved the hammer and thumbtacks Lois had provided. "We'll go home pretty quick, Frannie," I repeated.

"When I'm finished with the ice water," Frannie said—firmly, as if we'd made a bargain.

"When I've done what I have to do," I retorted with equal firmness.

I stubbornly took my time thumbtacking the cut-outs to the stair rail and ignored several petulant requests from Frannie that we go home *now*. I'd asked why she was in such an all-fired hurry, but she'd only answer tartly that she couldn't explain *here*. It would ruin the surprise.

I didn't find out what the surprise was until we were home. "Oh, no!" Frannie wailed as I pulled up in front of the garage. "Oh, I knew this would happen—I *knew* it! They're bound to be ruined!" She gestured in despair.

On the back porch just outside the kitchen door—and in full sunlight—were two crates of strawberries. I felt a little guilty for not having responded to Frannie's sense of urgency about getting home. "You should have told me," I said.

Frannie scrambled from the car. "The surprise for tomorrow," she lamented. "Strawberries dipped in white chocolate—it was going to be *so* elegant." She turned to me, accusingly. "You just *wouldn't* get finished and be ready to come home! And these strawberries can't be replaced. There aren't any other this size available anywhere—I phoned all over town. Angelo's Market was the only place, and they had to special-order them."

I picked up one of the crates of strawberries. They were the largest I'd ever seen. "Maybe they're still okay," I said. I tested one for firmness. "I don't think they've been in the sun too long."

Frannie inspected the strawberries. "They're hot. Hurry! We've got to put them in ice water." She fumbled with the back-door lock. "I just knew that delivery boy wouldn't have better sense than to . . . oh! They just *can't* be spoiled."

I set the strawberries on the kitchen table. Frannie dragged out a huge pot, we put water and ice cubes in it, and dumped in the berries.

When Vince arrived, she enlisted his help, too. By this time, she had prepared the white chocolate dip; it waited, warm, on the stove. We worked until late, but eventually all the strawberries had been dipped, placed in pleated cups of crisp white paper and carefully arranged on trays to cool. We stored as many as would fit in Frannie's refrigerator, the rest could go in mine.

I kept looking for an opportunity to talk with Vince, but we had no chance until we were carrying trays of strawberries up to my place. And, at that, I scarcely had a chance to get a word in edgewise; he was so intent on making sure I'd be safe.

"Emma, you gonna be okay?" he asked anxiously. "I mean, those nut-case letters—you got to take stuff like that seriously."

I assured him I'd be safe. "My door has a deadbolt. And I'll close and lock my windows tonight." Which was pointless, I thought. They were all on the second floor.

Vince was reluctant to be convinced.

"I could sleep in my car," he offered. "Out in the driveway, that way, I'd hear—"

"Nonsense!"

"Well, I got to do *something*."

I thought for a moment. "Well, there is one thing you could do."

"Yeah . . . sure."

"Tomorrow, at the gallery, would you check out the basement?" I explained about Old Sacramento's under-the-sidewalk passageways. "I think the chances are pretty slim that anyone would actually—"

"You don't want to let *nothing* go. Sure, I'll check it out."

"And, Vince, don't mention about those letters to Frannie. I haven't told her too much about them—or about Benny Podesta."

"Yeah," he said. "Some things she don't handle so good— no point in getting Frannie all riled up. And she's safe at home, got a real good security system."

Frannie'd had a top-of-the-line system installed a few years back. At the time, I thought she'd overspent. Now I thought differently.

Vince at last seemed to be satisfied that I would be safe enough; we went back to Frannie's for a late supper. Nonetheless, early the next morning when I opened the windows to let some fresh air into my stuffy apartment, Bulldog Valenti was in his car, fast asleep.

▽

4 1

W E HAD TO SCRAMBLE to get everything ready. It took a great deal of time to pack the strawberries—carefully separated with wads of tissue paper—in Frannie's Tupperware canisters. And she was relentlessly cheerful. "I suppose I did all that fretting for nothing," she said as we packed the last of the strawberries. "Gracious! Aren't you excited? Isn't this going to be a gorgeous day!"

At the last minute she insisted on bringing along the silver tray that's part of her coffee service. It's a monstrous thing—heavy, oval-shaped, and more than two feet long.

"We've already got the table and two chairs and a bunch of other stuff to bring home tonight," I reminded her.

"But the strawberries will display so magnificently on my silver tray!" She turned, appealing to Vince. "And you'll help us bring everything home, won't you."

"Sure thing," Vince said eagerly.

Another evening with Old Lonely, I thought. Tomorrow, Monday, he'd have to be back at work again. But I didn't want to consider the possibilities once he'd retired—an event now not all that far away.

At my suggestion, Frannie and Vince and the strawberries rode together. I watched as he gallantly escorted her from the porte cochere to his dusty Chevy; I followed in my truck.

190

The morning was already excessively warm. Today was going to be a scorcher, just as I'd anticipated.

At the gallery, the strawberries garnered even more praise than yesterday's cookies. Frannie, again in seventh heaven, carefully set out a dozen on the silver tray.

"The rest go in the refrigerator," she said. "I want them to stay *absolutely* cold as long as possible."

By the eleven o'clock opening time, Vince had left to pay a visit at the Sacramento police station, and Anne had made a late arrival—looking very attractive in a soft cream-colored blouse and rust slacks.

A small knot of curious tourists had assembled outside the gallery door. It would be a wonder, I thought, if they were attracted by the pennants; the little triangular flags hung limp in the still, hot air.

Brenda put me to work right away, helping to collect donations. I was to stand by the donation exhibit and offer Women Working Wonders brochures to folks who came within reach. Brenda had done this yesterday afternoon, drawing people's attention to the plastic tube full of money and checks and the red mark that indicated the day's goal. "Isn't it wonderful," she would say, "we've almost reached today's goal already." Then she would make a pitch about the goals of Jobs First.

That sort of thing was hardly my forte, but I consented to take a turn at it.

"Just keep smiling," Brenda told me, "and stand so they practically have to look through the donation tube to see your face." She inspected the tube. Yesterday's contributions had filled it well above the red *Day 1* mark. She scowled, then tipped the tube and pushed down the cash and checks until the donations were at the appropriate level. She winked at me. "You might just mention how happy we were to have reached yesterday's goal."

I did my best, but I wasn't happy in my work. Before long the sun worked its way around, and began to hit where I stood between the donation table and the window. Fortunately, Frannie wasn't in the sun yet, although she soon would be.

The best feature of the day was a phone call, about
half-past twelve, from Coretta. She was conscious, out of the
post-surgery recovery room, and planning to be home in a
day or two.

As far as I was concerned, another good piece of news was
that Jonathan Lee apparently had chosen not to show up.
Maybe, I thought, he'd decided that fame and fortune lay in
some other direction. Then I became uneasy, remembering
the idea Lois had put forward Friday night: Retribution
might be someone we knew.

Our intrepid reporter was intelligent enough to have
composed the letters. He might even try something like that
to scare us into giving the kind of interview he wanted. For
all I knew, he might be cold-blooded enough to have killed
Esther or attacked Coretta. But the motivation wasn't
there—too much risk for so small an advantage. The man
was a snot, but he wasn't a crazy.

Brenda came around, finally, to relieve me at my post. "It's
time we all had something to eat," she said. "This one's on
me." She fished in her purse. "How about sandwiches all
around?"

Anne appeared beside me. "I'll go get them," she volunteered. "Emma, will you help me?"

We took everyone's order and headed out into the heat of
Second Street, planning to get our food from a nearby
sandwich and ice cream shop. But a long line waited—just
to get in the door. Despite the heat, Old Sacramento seemed
to have drawn a bumper crop of tourists today.

"Let's duck under the freeway," I said. "We can go to the
coffee shop at the Holiday Inn."

Anne agreed.

"So what's with Tony?" I asked.

Anne raised her chin in a half-defiant manner. "It doesn't
matter any more," she said with exaggerated nonchalance.
"As far as I know, he's still in jail."

"Tony's in jail?"

"Since early Friday morning. The police picked him up at
a bar across the river in Broderick—drunk and fighting. He

hit someone pretty hard, I guess, and destroyed property.
There're a lot of charges."

We walked along in silence for a moment.

"He wanted me to post his bail," she said after a while.
She turned, facing me for the first time. "I had a choice
between spending all the money I had for that, or using it to
get into another apartment."

"And . . . ?"

"He'll serve his jail time and come home to an empty
place—probably with an eviction notice on the door for
non-payment of rent."

"Good for you!" We said no more about Tony.

I wondered—how early Friday morning had he been
picked up? *Someone we know.* Could he have attacked
Coretta? Perhaps. But he'd have to have killed Esther, too.
And Tony hardly seemed the type to listen to KXPR.

I told myself I was developing a first-class case of paranoia.

The Holiday Inn was busy, but nowhere near as crowded
as the restaurants in Old Sacramento. After a wait that was
only moderately long, Anne and I emerged from the coffee
shop laden with paper bags of sandwiches and cold drinks.
I'd accepted my share awkwardly at the cash register—cop-
ing with our change at the same time—and soon discovered
I'd have to re-sort my load.

I steered Anne toward the lobby. "Let's find a place to set
everything down. I'm afraid if I don't do this differently, the
drinks will spill."

We stopped outside the cocktail lounge and put our bags
on a low table. I glanced over at the lounge entrance. Just
inside, seated at the bar, was Al Friedman, doing a classic
barstool lovey-dovey act. He was with a dark-haired woman
in a red dress—a *hot patootsie* if I ever saw one.

"Oh, no!" Anne exclaimed softly.

Brenda's husband and the woman were wrapped up in
each other, oblivious to the world. As we watched, his hand
roamed up and down her red-sheathed fanny. He gave her a
little pat, then a pinch. She giggled.

Anne seemed to be in a state of shock—dumbfounded and

dismayed. Or disillusioned, maybe. She'd often talked about how wonderful Brenda's husband was to let her have so much freedom to do what she wanted with Jobs First.

I understood now his odd reaction when I'd invited him to go hiking. No wonder he'd been so flustered! I'd said something about his *collecting*. I meant geologic specimens—no telling what he thought I meant.

I re-assembled the lunch packages as quickly as I could. "Let's get out of here," I said.

Anne and I were silent until we neared the gallery.

"Let's not tell the others," Anne suggested.

I agreed.

▽

42

"O<small>H!"</small> F<small>RANNIE</small> <small>EXCLAIMED</small> <small>THE</small> minute Anne and I walked through the door. "Have you got cold drinks? I'm so hot and thirsty!"

Her face was red, little rivulets of sweat streaked her bosom. She dabbed herself with a Kleenex, unmindful that she was smearing traces of pink and white—strawberry and melted white chocolate.

"Come on, Frannie," I said. "It's cooler in the back room."

"I can take over for you here," Anne said.

Frannie protested that she shouldn't leave, there were still so many strawberries to be sold. But Anne and I persisted.

"Don't worry, I'll get them sold," Anne said.

Frannie capitulated. I steered her through the gallery, distributing sandwiches and cold drinks as I went. She plopped onto the couch in the back room and took her first eager gulps of the iced tea I'd brought.

I decided I'd best stay and keep an eye on her.

I started in on my lunch. Frannie, despite a polite expression of gratitude for her chicken sandwich, took only one disinterested bite. She had a few more long, thirsty sips of tea, then leaned back and closed her eyes; within moments she was asleep.

I briefly considered going out front to see what needed

doing, then decided to relax and enjoy my lunch. I was working on the second half of my sandwich when Vince showed up.

"Jeez!" He exclaimed, too engrossed in what he wanted to tell me to notice Frannie. "Those guys up at Carson City—"

"Shhh!" I pointed at her.

"Sorry," Vince whispered.

I motioned him to follow me. We held a conference in the mezzanine storeroom, Vince expostulating vehemently about the reluctance of the Carson City police, and the local Bunco squad as well, to take further action—no complaint had been filed.

"How about the mail fraud angle?" I asked. I was staring out the window at the alley below.

"Yeah," Vince said, brightening considerably. "The Postal Inspection guys. I was going to go see them anyways." He launched into a discussion about what he anticipated would be the intricacies of procedure the Postal Inspection Service would follow.

Out in the alley a derelict shambled by, in one hand a ragged cloth sack—it apparently had something heavy in it. He was a small-faced man, with shaggy eyebrows, his skin the color of mahogany from the combined effects of grime and sun, and deeply creased. He wore an oversize dark shirt, with more clothing underneath; his hair was tucked under a watch cap, greasy and motheaten.

I thought of the lank, filthy hair the cap probably concealed, the vermin his clothing no doubt harbored. My skin crawled.

"Postal Service will get the Muellers the long, slow way," Vince said, "but I sure wish someone would file a complaint. You don't suppose Frannie—"

"Don't even ask," I said. "Let the Postal Service catch up with them eventually." Or at least with Carl, I thought. Rachel hadn't gone to Carson City, apparently. Maybe she'd found out about the bank accounts that didn't include her. I wondered what kind of scam they each would work if they were no longer a team. But I didn't trouble Bulldog Valenti with the thought that Rachel might have escaped his net.

"With scams, that's always the problem," Vince said. "Too many people are like Frannie. When they been taken in, they don't want to talk about it."

I held firm on the don't-ask-Frannie point. I saw no reason to drag her through all that humiliation just to put the collar on Mueller a little sooner.

Vince said he had to go out again. Lois had asked him to buy blocks of ice to put in front of the fans. "It won't make that much difference," he explained, "but Brenda told Lois to do it because people will *think* they're cooler." He shrugged, then wiped perspiration from his brow. "When I get done with the ice, I'll go downstairs and check that basement."

We abandoned the stifling heat of the mezzanine room, Vince to fetch ice, me to finish my lunch.

I chewed thoughtfully on my pastrami, and wondered about the threat in those letters. *I will now descend upon all of you.* The Women Working Wonders exhibit would soon be over—only a few hours to go.

I looked over at Frannie's sleeping form. She wasn't one of us—not a *harlot.* But how far would the killer go?

I remembered, uneasily, the bum I'd seen from the mezzanine. Old Sacramento was a skid row a few decades ago. Back then Second Street was called Two Street; its unfortunate denizens swarmed among cheap restaurants and bath houses, sleazy bars and brothels, rabbit-warren hotels. Why hadn't it registered with me? A derelict. Here. Now. He was totally out of place.

I hurried up the stairs to have another look out the window. I saw nothing but the vacant alley, its sun-drenched pavement and deep shade punctuated here and there by garbage cans and empty doorways. Still uneasy, I returned to my lunch.

I'd finished and just started to pick up the wrappings when Kitty came into the back room. "Anne says she needs more strawberries up front."

I made shushing motions, pointing to Frannie, and then indicated the refrigerator.

Frannie opened her eyes. "Strawberries," she said. "Keep most of them back here, they can't be in the sun too long." She smiled weakly. "Just like me." And then she was asleep again.

Kitty left, with about a dozen strawberries. But she came right back. "Anne wants the rest of the strawberries, too," she whispered, "to make a better sales display."

I wondered if putting out all the strawberries at once was wise, but decided not to interfere.

When Kitty had left I retrieved Frannie's uneaten sandwich and put it in the refrigerator. Then I collected the leavings from my lunch, and looked around for a wastebasket. There was none. I'd seen a garbage can in the alley, just outside. I put a hand to the deadbolt and was about to open the alley door when I decided I should also collect everyone else's lunch wrappings.

As soon as I emerged from the back room, Anne caught my eye and signaled me over. "Look," she said with obvious pride. "What do you think of that?"

She'd taken the fluted paper wrappings off the strawberries, and massed them together in the shape of a heart. It did look enticing, with the pink and white strawberries set off by the deep rose color of the linen napkin on Frannie's silver tray. But the chocolate was already filmed with a coating of moisture, and strawberry juice stains showed in a few places along the edge of the heart.

Anne must have read the misgiving in my face.

"I put them close together on purpose," she said defensively. "That way they'll keep each other cool."

Not for long, I thought. The sales table was in full sunlight.

I wanted to say something—no matter that I'd resolved not to interfere. But at that moment Vince walked in, carrying a huge block of ice on his shoulder. His arrival was greeted with cheers and clapping; he grinned self-consciously.

Al Friedman walked in.

I stared, flabbergasted. He caught Brenda's eye and gave her a friendly wave, then started examining a display of quilts along one wall. He apparently was an old hand at deception—his expression was calm, his eyes behind the wire-rimmed glasses bland and totally innocent.

"Some nerve," Anne muttered.

I glanced uneasily at Brenda, who was less than ten feet away and happened to be looking in our direction. "Let them work it out," I said quietly. I put a smile on my face. "Keep up the good work with the strawberry sales," I added in a louder voice.

At that moment Jonathan Lee walked in through the gallery's front door. Despite the heat, he looked clean and crisp—still the ultimate *preppie*, in a camp shirt and Bermuda shorts. Inevitably, he had his tape recorder with him. He flashed me an ingenuous smile, smoothed back the lock of hair from his forehead, and headed straight for Brenda.

Unwilling to tangle with Lee, I hurriedly finished collecting lunch leavings and headed for the back room.

Lois was there, standing irresolutely in front of the refrigerator, arms crossed and hands hugging her elbows. I gave her an inquisitive look.

She shrugged, still clinging to her elbows. "Case of nerves," she said. She forced a smile, let her arms drop to her sides and expelled a breath. "You caught me at it."

"I've had some of the same feelings myself," I admitted. I started for the alley door.

"Oh, I don't think you should go out there," she said quickly.

"Why not?"

"There's a man—I started to go outside a minute ago. I know he's just a derelict, but when I saw him I got this feeling . . ."

"A guy in dark clothes and a watch cap?"

She nodded.

"Let's go up the mezzanine and have a look," I said.

We scrambled up the stairs.

The derelict was there. He stood immobile in the shadows of a doorway adjacent to the restaurant fence, his cloth satchel on the doorsill beside his feet.

$\triangledown$

43

"STAY BY THE WINDOW and keep an eye on him," I told Lois. "I'll go find Vince. I think he's in the basement."

The door was unlocked, the hanging bulb over the stairs still swinging. I was about to start down the stairs when the commotion started out front.

"Oh! No!" Anne wailed. She held up one of the big strawberries and squeezed the white chocolate shell, releasing a torrent of bright pink juice. "No!" she wailed again as another strawberry collapsed into dribbly red mush.

I turned again, took a step or two down the rickety stairs. I thought I could see a light moving in the dim recesses of the basement. "Vince!" I called. No answer. He probably was inspecting the under-the-sidewalk area at the front of the building—too far away to hear me. I started down to get him.

Anne passed behind me in the hallway, carrying Frannie's silver tray and its burden of rotted strawberries. Then I head her unlock the door to the alley.

I leaped back up the stairs and saw her, tray in hand, silhouetted by the alley's glare.

"Anne," I hissed. She turned, confused.

I dashed forward, pulled her back.

"Why are you . . . ?"

I slammed the deadbolt into place. "He's out there—Lois and I saw him."

Anne shook her head in bewilderment, the comprehension slowly dawned. "*Retribution,*" she whispered.

"Lois," I called up the stairs. "What's he doing?"

"You scared him—I think he's going to leave."

Frannie woke up with a start. "What!" She blinked, looking at Anne. "Oh, my goodness—the strawberries!"

"Phone the police," Lois shouted down the stairs. "It's him all right. He had a gasoline can in that sack. He was dabbing it on his clothes. Hurry! He's leaving. Oh, damn! He's leaving!"

I started toward the phone, then heard the unmistakable sound of the alley-door deadbolt being pulled back.

Anne, already outside, turned back, a smile on her face. "I'll just be a minute," she called with false cheerfulness, "I'll be back as soon as I've gotten rid of these." She stepped briskly into the alley.

"My strawberries!" Frannie keened.

"Wait!" Lois called. "I think . . . he's coming back."

Again I started for the phone.

"My God!" Lois cried. "He's got a wrench—he's going for her."

I ran outside. The man was closing fast on Anne, the wrench in his upraised hand. He froze when he saw me. I dashed forward, grabbed the tray from Anne, and slung it at him with all my might.

I'd done it just right, caught him at the ankles and knocked his feet out from under him. He landed on the pavement in a shower of rotting strawberries, howling in pain. The tray clanged on the paving stones, the wrench hit too. I rushed over to kick it away, then took hold of the man's ankles and pulled up as hard as I could. He struggled and slid in the pink mire.

From inside the gallery came a terrible crashing sound, and muffled shouts from Vince. Frannie screamed.

I hung on to my struggling captive.

"Be still or I'll shoot!" It was Lois, beside me, her voice

gruff and almost unrecognizable. She held a pistol in both hands.

He stared at her, the whites of his eyes standing out in stark fear. Or rage. I couldn't tell which. Brenda rushed past me, collected Frannie's silver tray and held it over his head. "Stay where you are," she commanded.

I tightened my grip on his ankles. He glared, eyes darting from one to another of us.

"Kitty's calling the police," Brenda told us.

By now people were emerging from the gallery's back door, murmuring and questioning; they stopped, keeping their distance from our tableau.

"Kitty's also calling an ambulance," Brenda added. "For Vince. The stairway collapsed."

I knew something serious must have happened, or he would have been out here. I hoped someone was taking care of him.

People were still crowding out from the gallery, spreading in both ways along the alley but keeping a distance. More curious onlookers approached from both ends of the alley.

Al Friedman emerged from the crowd and stood tentatively beside Brenda. She kept a firm grip on the tray, her attention focused on Retribution. We must have been a sight.

Behind me, in the crowd, Frannie wailed to someone about her strawberries. And I could pick out Jonathan Lee's voice, talking into his tape recorder—he'd have his big story, one way or another.

We waited.

At last we heard sirens, and then a police car screeched to a stop at one end of the alley. At the same time, in the gallery, I could hear a stir and official-sounding requests—"Step aside" and "Police, let us through."

Two officers from the car in the alley reached us first. I lowered our captive's feet to the ground. Brenda lowered the tray; Lois put away her gun.

"Police officers," one of the policeman announced. "Move slowly," he commanded. "Get to your feet. Hold your hands behind the back of your head."

Retribution complied, eyes glaring defiance. Pink slime streaked his face; his outer shirt was soaked with it. He stood stock still and ramrod straight, displaying a degree of self-possession and dignity that astonished me.

The officer stepped forward and handcuffed him.

Quite deliberately, Retribution spat at us. "Harlots!"

The voice was nothing more than a hoarse whisper, but it wasn't a man's voice.

I stepped forward for a closer look. The mahogany skin and deep lines were makeup, the shaggy eyebrows as well. Retribution glared straight into my face; I reached up and pulled off the watch cap. A mass of dark auburn hair tumbled downward, a parchment-pale forehead was revealed. Even before she pulled off the false eyebrows, I knew it was Rachel Mueller.

"Harlots!" Her eyes gleamed, roved over each of us. "Harlots—all of you!"

"Oh, my!" Frannie gasped.

Rachel glared at Frannie, then back at us—the fierce stare at odds with the comical effect of the half-parchment, half-grime face with its pale ellipses marking the absent eyebrows.

"The evil you have wrought—unnatural women! You are abominations . . . filth!"

She moved as if to raise her arms, but they were confined by the handcuffs. "I am the spirit," she intoned—a low, intense growl. "I am Retribution." Her voice rose, her eyes huge as she stared about her, her body pulled up to full height. "I will overcome the evil you have created. I will rule with God for what I do." By now she was shouting. "God said so. It's in Revelations. To the one who overcomes, I give the right to sit with me on my throne."

The officer beckoned to his partner.

Rachel laughed, threw back her head. "I will become a pillar in the temple of my God! I will eat from the tree of life, in the paradise of God!" She glared at us with scorn. "He will dash you to pieces like pottery."

They began leading her away.

"Woe unto them that decree unrighteous decrees," Rachel

shouted back at us. "Wickedness burneth as the fire. The hour of your destruction is come!"

Dear God! She believed it.

All this time, she must have believed everything she was saying.

$\triangledown$

44

IT TOOK HOURS TO get things sorted out at the police station, but finally it was all over. I don't know why I did it—I'm no hostess—but I invited everybody to come to my place.

"What a wonderful idea," Lois crooned. "Exactly the right thing to do. This has been such a tragedy—we'll transform it into a positive event."

"A party," Kitty said. "Right on! I'm starved."

Frannie fell in with the plans immediately. "There's a new deli over on Twenty-first Street. They have the most marvelous prosciutto. Emma and I can stop by. Let's see . . . prosciutto and some good cheeses, and oh!—Greek olives, and some of those little peppers . . ." She fished in her purse, and brought out a note pad and pencil. "French bread, of course . . . pasta salad . . ."

I was happy to see her perking up again. She'd been thoroughly upset about Rachel Mueller—as much as anything frightened, I supposed, that someone she'd been convinced was a *nice lady* turned out to be so fiercely deranged.

"Hey! Leave something for the rest of us," Kitty said. "I'll take care of paper plates, and plastic silverware and glasses, napkins—all that sort of stuff."

"I've got some champagne back at the gallery," Lois said. "I had it in the refrigerator for tonight, in any event."

"I'll bring soft drinks," Anne put in quickly.

"Sure thing," I added. "And I've got plenty of coffee."

Brenda grinned. "I'll bring that plastic tube full of donations. We can count the money—we're going to have plenty to celebrate."

Frannie and I led the way back to my place, with suitable detours at Lois's gallery and at the Twenty-first Street deli. We must have made quite a parade, pulling into Frannie's driveway one after another. Velma Patterson stood by her backyard fence, garden hose in hand, gaping.

I imagined the encounter with Velma tomorrow. First would come her leading question: "Well, you certainly had a lot of company last night." Then my answer: "Yes, I certainly did," after which I would say no more. I was rather looking forward to it.

I led our food and champagne laden parade up my stairs, and unlocked the front door—cheerfully flinging it wide open.

I'd left my place buttoned up tight; it was hot as a furnace. I hurried to fling open windows and let in the evening breeze.

Sourpuss confronted me, jumping up on the kitchen counter and staring at me with his most reproachful gaze. "Things are almost back to normal, my friend," I whispered to him. "You'll get your food as soon as I start a pot of coffee."

Frannie, puffing from the climb up my apartment stairs, began unwrapping and dishing up the deli food, spreading it buffet-style along the kitchen counter—Brenda having appropriated my kitchen table, where she and Kitty were already sorting the donation money into stacks of checks and bills of various denominations.

"Have you got some butter?" Frannie asked. "Let's see, mayonnaise, too. I bought some *good* mustard, two kinds, at the deli, and . . . now where did I put it?" She trailed off, happily arranging our feast. I set out butter, mayonnaise and some other trimmings, and gave Sourpuss his supper.

Brenda announced that she'd brought Frannie's cookie and strawberry money, too. "Who wants to count that?"

Anne volunteered.

"I'll make the hospital calls," Lois said. "Vince first, and then Coretta."

She had good news when she'd finished her phone calls. "First," she smiled. "Coretta will be coming home tomorrow." Everyone clapped and cheered. "And, second, Vince will be fine. They've just finished putting the cast on his leg." More cheering and clapping. "They've checked him over—the leg *was* the worst of it but they're going to keep him overnight for observation. The poor man! That stairway. I should have known."

"Your landlord should have known," Kitty put in. "You could sue his socks off for that."

"We'll talk about nothing contentious tonight," Lois said firmly. She smiled. "Now—who's going to help me open this champagne?"

We had a number of toasts to drink.

"To the memory of Esther Vajic, a good friend and a wonderful worker," Brenda said solemnly.

The mood soon lightened. We toasted the success of the fundraising event, and then Coretta's recovery, and Vince's.

"Such a *wonderful* friend," Lois proclaimed, shaking her head. "Emma, you just don't know how lucky you are." She sighed prodigiously.

Frannie echoed Lois's sigh. I squirmed, trying to think of a way to change the subject.

"Hey," Kitty said. "We need a toast to the capture of *Retribution*." She giggled. "A slippery character at the end, if I ever saw one!"

That set everyone off. Brenda began teasing Lois about being a *pistol-packing-mama*, which is the title to an old song.

I sat back, watching the hilarity. None of us wanted any serious talk now about Rachel Mueller.

Lois had given us a psychologist's explanation when we were at the police station—it was full of words like *projection, compulsion, delusional behavior*. What it boiled down to was that Rachel had gone overboard with her religious beliefs, placing more and more restrictions on herself as a *good Christian woman* and becoming more and more angry at other women who didn't do the same. With her marriage to Carl Mueller, she saw herself as the perfect helpmate for the perfect doer of God's will—and he probably saw her as the perfect person to take advantage of. She seemed to have some conflicts about sex, too. For instance, she equated female independence with sexual immorality.

"I think she was pushed over the edge," Lois had mused, "by her increasing awareness that Carl, the man she'd given herself to sexually, was not the man she imagined him . . . absolutely needed him . . . to be. When one piece of the delusional belief system begins to be suspect, the entire fantasy is endangered. She sought to keep her delusions intact by escaping more and more into what she saw as a battle against *evil*, a battle she believed to be sanctioned by the Bible."

"And then it wouldn't matter any more that her husband was an ordinary con man," Kitty suggested. "God was going to reward her."

We'd all been silent for a while.

"I feel sorry for her," Anne said.

"Not as sorry as I feel for Coretta," Brenda snapped, "or Esther." That had ended our police station conversation about Rachel.

I concentrated on eating my food and watching the festivities.

Frannie jumped up, and, pointing at Lois, began singing the first verse to *Pistol-Packing Mama*. She waved her arms as if conducting a songfest, encouraging the others to sing.

I stole a look at Sourpuss. He'd retreated earlier to the bedroom and sat watching from the doorway. Now, as everyone began singing, he turned and slunk under my bed.

I was glad to see *us girls* having fun. There was plenty of work in store. Returning everything from the gallery exhibit, and then patching up the office—we'd done nothing but retrieve a few items from the reception room, and I'd nailed a piece of plywood over the workroom door.

I'd help Brenda and the others, I thought, but I didn't

want to become a regular Jobs First activist. Parading around
with signs and staging protests wasn't my cup of tea—nor
was getting arrested. But they could use my help from time
to time—for stray repairs, or maybe when a truck was
needed.

I joined in with the singing. Frannie was dancing, a little
jig. "Lay that pistol down," she sang breathlessly. "Pistol
packing ma—ma, la-aaay that pistol down!" She collapsed
onto my rocking chair.

Kitty and Brenda finally finished counting money. Both
the cookie sale and the fundraising event had been smash
financial successes.

It was late before we were saying our last good-byes in the
driveway.

Lois and Frannie had been having a private conversation,
a development I regarded with some apprehension. "When
Vince retires," Lois announced, nodding her head in a
meaningful way toward me, "I want to hire him as a security
guard on weekends—I think some of my business neighbors
might be willing to chip in." Frannie smiled blissfully, her
cat-that-swallowed-the-canary look. "And when he's working in Old Sacramento, he can stay at my house," she added.

I might have known. *Double jeopardy.*

I headed back up the stairs.

Sourpuss was on the drainboard, licking the last of the
butter in my butter dish.

I yelled at him; he dashed into the bedroom.

Things were back to normal. Almost.